MURDER AT THE BRITISH MUSEUM

THE KITTY WORTHINGTON MYSTERIES, BOOK 12

MAGDA ALEXANDER

HEARTS AFIRE PUBLISHING

CHAPTER 1

LONDON 1925

A NEW YEAR

*T*he fire crackled in the drawing room hearth of Worthington House, my parents' home, its warmth a welcome heat against the January chill. Mother had once more arranged a wonderful Sunday supper for family and friends. A return to normalcy after the burial of Robert's brother.

Barely two weeks into the new year, he'd sadly succumbed to his heart's complaint. The entire family and many of our friends had joined us in the sad journey to Chipping Bliss where we'd interred his remains in Castle Rutledge's family crypt. After the solemnity of that funeral, this evening was exactly what Robert needed.

I'd been wandering around the drawing room thanking our family and friends for their support of Robert during this sad time. But I'd neglected him long enough. The poor darling was sitting by himself on a sofa looking rather forlorn. It was time I rejoined him. Putting on my brightest smile, I settled next to him. "A penny for your thoughts."

"I was contemplating my schedule for tomorrow. A meeting with the solicitor followed by one with your father."

"And you're worried about it?" The immensity of his new responsibilities as the new Lord Rutledge weighed heavily on him, so much so he was constantly scribbling something or other in the notebook he always carried with him.

"Not worried exactly. Concerned about being thorough."

I squeezed his hand. "You are, darling. Think of all those innumerable lists you've created. And you know you can depend on Father and Ned for financial advice. They would never steer you wrong."

"I'm extremely grateful for their guidance. Still, there's a vast amount of information I must learn."

"And you will, just not all at once. As the saying goes, Rome wasn't built in a day." The Rutledge interests spanned continents—from Asia to Europe to America. The enormity of it boggled the mind. At least the investments were in the hands of Worthington & Son, Father's investment firm. So that was one thing Robert did not have to worry about.

But given the breadth of his holdings in India, he would need to travel there to acquaint himself with the interests his grandfather had acquired over a century ago. It would not be any time soon, though. He planned to wait until the latter part of the year when the weather would be more favorable.

His brow cleared up as he gazed at me. "You'll have to remind me of that when I grow tiresome."

"Oh, I will." I grinned. "Don't you worry. And you're never tiresome." The last thing I wanted was for him to be so absorbed by his new responsibilities, he neglected himself. At least he wouldn't have to worry about his chief detective inspector duties. He'd taken temporary leave from those responsibilities to acquaint himself with the Rutledge estate and everything that entailed. Though Robert had not said as much, I suspected he would eventually resign his post at Scotland Yard.

"I also have a meeting with Salisbury at four tomorrow," Robert continued.

"As in the Marquess of? The leader of the House of Lords?"

"Yes. He wants to discuss my political views."

"Heavens!" Salisbury should have allowed Robert time to mourn his brother, but seemingly political maneuvering did not allow for such a thing.

"Exactly."

"Poor darling," I said threading my hand through his. "I'll have Cook prepare your favorite supper tomorrow so you have something to look forward to."

He raised my hand to his lips and kissed it. "I'll be thinking of it while I'm in the meeting with him."

"I'm sure you'll manage well enough," my sister Margaret said approaching us. As she took a seat on the wingback chair across from us, she cradled her rounded belly with both hands. She was due to give birth in but a few weeks.

Robert offered her a wry smile. "Thank you. The management of it all is a great responsibility. I intend to do my best."

"And you most certainly will," I added. "You'll have plenty of people to assist you—Father and Ned, your solicitor and the estate stewards. And, of course, me if you wished for my help."

Mother, who'd quietly wandered toward us, nodded in agreement. "Quite right, my dear. You'll find your footing soon enough, Robert. Most men in your position begin with small matters before handling larger ones."

Father, who had been mostly silent, sipping his port, joined our group. "You might want to take some advice from those who have been managing estates for years. Visit other landowners. See what methods they employ."

Robert exhaled. "It is all a bit daunting. I had my life well in hand, my career on a steady path, and now—" He shook his head. "I knew this day would come. I just hoped it wouldn't be so soon."

Margaret, looking as though she might burst at any moment, shifted in her seat. "Life rarely waits until one is ready, dear Robert. I, for instance, am expected to give birth in February, but I'm quite certain this babe means to arrive any day now."

Most everyone laughed. Sebastian, however, found no mirth in his wife's statement. "Maybe we should return home?" he suggested.

Margaret reached for his hand. "I was joking, Sebastian. The midwife assured me it will be several weeks before your son or daughter makes their way into the world."

"Very well," he said, his eye twitching. Since New Year's Day, he'd grown increasingly more agitated. For his sake, I hoped Margaret would soon deliver their infant. Otherwise, he was likely to suffer a nervous collapse.

"Speaking of new beginnings," my brother Richard said, "I have an announcement to make."

"Do you, my dear?" Mother's grin resembled the Cheshire Cat's. Whatever Richard was to say she was fully cognizant of it.

Richard straightened slightly, clearly pleased. "I've been offered a position as a lecturer on Egyptian Antiquities at the British Museum. Since the opening of King Tut's tomb, they've seen a surge of interest in Egyptology. They believe my lectures will be well attended."

"Well attended?" I said. "It'll be standing room only. Just you wait and see. You'll probably have to turn away people at the door."

"Especially the ladies," Margaret joked with a grin.

A round of laughter circled the room. She wasn't wrong, though. Richard had extensive archeological experience as he'd spent the last several years on Egyptian digs. It didn't hurt he'd inherited the good looks of the Worthington clan. And, when he chose to exert himself, he could be quite charming.

As Mother and Father gazed fondly upon their son, a chorus of congratulations rang out across the room

"It's a remarkable opportunity," Richard continued. "Of course, it means I shall be spending a great deal more time in London, but I believe it's a worthy endeavor." A few months ago, he'd arrived home deathly ill with malaria. Once he'd recovered, his physician had told him in no uncertain terms that if he returned to Egypt, sooner or later, he would have a relapse. And without access to the excellent care available in London, he might die.

Predictably, Richard had rebelled against this restriction. So much so, our parents had worried sick he would not heed his doctor's advice and return to Egypt. But thankfully, this wonderful new opportunity had been found for him. Even more important, it was one he was excited about.

"The British Museum is fortunate to have you," Father said. "With all the charlatans out there peddling half-truths and exaggerated claims, it is good to know the public will have access to genuine scholarship."

"As long as the work is fulfilling, that's all that matters," Robert added. "And you, Richard, are the most well-rounded scholar I know." Indeed, he was as he'd also majored in archaeology at Oxford. Combined with his practical experience, it made him a truly unique lecturer.

Richard inclined his head in thanks. But before he could speak further, the conversation took another turn.

"Has there been any word of Hollingsworth?" Margaret

inquired. At the end of our last investigation, Hollingsworth had announced he would be taking a holiday.

Mother sighed. "He's left England for warmer climes, though where exactly, no one knows. Not even Mellie." She glanced at Hollingsworth's sister. "Isn't that right, dear?"

Mellie shrugged. "Not so much as a scribble." Seemingly, she didn't care about the lack of communication from her brother, but I knew better. Deep down, she was hurting.

"He made arrangements before departing," Father said. "He entrusted Mellie's well-being to your mother and the management of her funds to Worthington & Son."

"What about his sailing ship?" Margaret asked.

"He placed it on dry dock." Father's tone seemed to signal an end to that particular discussion. Last thing he wanted, indeed all of us wanted, was to continue a conversation bound to disturb Mellie.

I glanced at Robert, who looked thoughtful. "It does seem rather mysterious," I whispered. "Leaving England without a proper explanation, even to his sister?"

"He has always been a restless soul," Robert said. "Whatever compelled him to leave, it was not a decision made lightly."

"Well," Margaret said, heaving a sigh. "Wherever Hollingsworth has gone, I hope he finds whatever he's seeking. As for me, I'd very much like to seek my bed."

"Yes, of course, my dear," Sebastian quickly agreed helping her to her feet.

With the evening winding down, Robert and I took our leave as well. Stepping outside into the cold night air, Robert took my hand, his fingers threading through mine. "Thank you, Catherine. This evening was exactly what I needed."

I leaned into him, pressing my cheek against his shoulder. "You'll find your way, my love. And I'll be beside you, every step of the journey."

He kissed the top of my head. "I don't doubt it for a moment."

As we stepped into his Rolls-Royce, I glanced back at the warm glow of Worthington House, a beacon against the darkness. No matter what changes came our way, one thing remained certain—family would always be our anchor.

CHAPTER 2

LIFE MARCHES ON

A week later, Margaret's prediction came true. Her babe decided to make its way into the world. Since I had not experienced childbirth, I was not allowed to attend the birthing. Instead, I waited in the Wynchcombe House drawing room along with Lily, who was fairly vibrating with excitement at the thought of becoming an aunt.

While we drank tea and coffee, Robert, Ned, Father, and Richard spent their time fortifying a frantic Sebastian with whiskey.

Several hours later, the midwife arrived with the news we'd been expecting. Sebastian barely waited for her last word before rushing up the stairs two at a time. Sometime later, he returned grinning ear to ear. "I have a son! We named him Thomas Edward after both grandfathers."

"That's a grand name. Congratulations," Father said, patting his son-in-law in the back. "How's Margaret?"

"Brilliant!" Sebastian's eyes filled with tears. "She's remarkable."

"Yes, that she is," Father agreed, a note of relief in his voice. Although Margaret had the best midwife and physician to be found in all of London, there could always be dire consequences. Even in this day and age, childbirth was a perilous affair.

Lily embraced her brother, "Congratulations! I'm so happy for you!"

"Thank you, dear sister. You're an aunt!"

"I intend to take full advantage of that status."

"Please do," he said, hugging her back.

While the men crowded around Sebastian, pounding his back and congratulating him on his ordeal (?), Lily and I headed to the duchess's bedchamber.

We found Margaret barely awake as we entered the room, but she was all smiles as she cradled the small bundle in her arms. Clearly, she'd come through with flying colors. "Kitty, Lily, come and see my son."

As we approached, she brushed back the blanket wrapped around him so we could see his face. "His eyes are blue, but Mother says that might change."

"He's a handsome boy, Margaret," I said even though the babe resembled a scrunched-up peanut.

"He's beautiful," Lady Lily exclaimed. Clearly, the words of a deluded aunt.

"Indeed, he is," Mother replied. We were only allowed to remain a few minutes as Margaret needed her rest. After whispering a few words to Margaret, Mother brushed a kiss on her head. "I'll visit in the morning, shall I?"

"Yes, please do," Margaret whispered back. "Thank you for everything. I don't think I could have done this without your presence."

"Nonsense, dear. You would have done just fine. Now put him to your breast. He needs to start suckling right away."

"Here, I'll help," the midwife said as Lily, Mother, and I quietly quit the room.

～

AFTER THE EXCITEMENT of the Marquis of Thropplethorpe's birth, the babe's courtesy title, I would have loved to say that life returned to normal. But it was not to be.

Robert, now busier than ever, needed to meet with his estate manager at Rutledge Castle to discuss not only that property but the distillery and brewery. When we'd visited the castle back in October, we'd learned the family brewed and distilled its own whiskey ale, selling it under the name Rutledge Reserve.

Due to the poor health of Robert's brother, that part of the estate had been sorely neglected. Not only was some of the equipment in need of repair, but new machinery needed to be purchased. Robert, being Robert, wanted to learn everything about the brewery and the distillery before he approved the expenses.

The morning of his departure, I stood alongside him in the foyer while he donned his coat, hat and gloves. Hudson, who was doing double duty as valet and chauffeur, was waiting at the curb in the Rolls-Royce. He would drive Robert to Victoria Station.

I fought back tears as I said goodbye to him. "I'll miss you terribly. Don't stay away too long."

Realizing the state I was in, he turned to our butler, "Mister Black, we need a moment of privacy."

"Of course, milord." After signaling the footman next to him, they quietly exited the foyer.

"Sweetheart." He brushed a tear from my cheek. "I'll be back before you know it."

"Yes, of course." I shook my head. "I'm sorry I'm being a ninny. It's just . . . "

He gazed at me a question mark in his eyes. And then he realized what I'd been hesitant to say. "It's the first time we've been away from each other since we wed."

"Yes." I grabbed his lapels and kissed him. "Now go, before I totally disgrace myself."

"Not just yet." Crooking a finger, he lifted my chin and kissed me with all the passion I'd come to know. Once we came up for air, he said, "I love you, Catherine."

"And I love you." I gently pushed him away. "Now go."

"Here." He tucked his handkerchief into my hand. "Something to remind you of me."

The handkerchief smelled like his cologne. The devil! He knew what that did to me. I forced myself to wait until he slipped out the door before inhaling his scent. I had some pride after all.

I never imagined that I would need him so desperately in my life, that I would ache to breathe him in, that my days would not be complete unless we came together at night. Sometimes I gazed across the dining room table and wondered how he'd become such a vital part of me. Was I losing myself or gaining something wonderful?

"Lady Rutledge, milady." The voice that broke into my reverie belonged to our butler. He'd returned to his post.

"Yes, Mister Black."

"Would you like your motorcar driven around?"

Fully back in the here and now, I weighed his question and decided against it. "No, thank you. If you could have James hail a taxicab for me. The weather is still much too cold for me to travel in the roadster."

"Of course, milady."

In no time at all, James had a taxicab waiting for me at the curb. After donning my coat, hat, and gloves, I stepped out of the townhouse and into the vehicle.

"Where to, ma'am?" The driver asked.

I gave him the address of the Ladies of Distinction Detective Agency. As busy as I'd been with the funeral and its aftermath, Emma, my business partner had had to shoulder the burden of the agency by herself. But now I was free and eager to return to my duties. The busier I was, the less I would miss Robert. Or so I hoped.

I arrived at the agency to discover my wish was to be granted. Emma was knee deep in new enquiries.

"We are busy. How wonderful," I said as I joined her in her office for our weekly discussion. "Tell me all about it."

"Well, to begin with, the aristocracy and the upper class are returning from their estates. The start of the season is but a few weeks away, after all. And other enquiries don't dry up. Case in point." She held up a folder. "Sir Frederick has asked us to look into yet another matter."

The barrister who'd represented Robert when he'd been accused of murder had been so impressed with my investigative skills that he'd started sending enquiries our way—everything from gathering evidence, conducting surveillance, performing background checks on witnesses, and uncovering information that might not be readily available to him. Essentially, we'd become an extension of his legal team.

We appreciated the business for it kept our agency busy during those times when the upper crust abandoned London at the end of the season. But the increase in our workload required us to work an inordinate number of hours from February through the end of August.

"Assign whatever you deem best to me. With Robert's duties at Rutledge Castle taking up so much of his time, I'd rather be working than sitting at home twiddling my thumbs."

"Oh, don't worry. I have several enquiries set aside for you." She patted a pile of folders.

"Such as?"

"Lady Turner wants someone to investigate several suitors for her daughter. Lady Holland is missing some jewelry. She suspects her sister-in-law. There's bad blood there. And the most interesting one of all,—" she pushed a folder toward me "—Lady Fallon claims her daughter left home to join a cult. She wants us to extricate her."

"Good heavens!" I picked up the folder and quickly perused the information. "The daughter—"

"Miranda."

"Why, she's only seventeen. How did that happen?"

"That's what you'll need to find out."

"Fine." I took the three case folders. "What have you assigned to Mellie?" Hollingsworth's sister had been working for us for the last month. She was very bright and more than eager to learn. Initially, we'd asked her to shadow Lady Aurelia, our Assistant Lady Detective. But as busy as we were expecting to be, we would need her to pull her own weight.

"Well, Sir Frederick's current enquiry requires someone to go through newspaper archives and court records to find information about several witnesses and the victim. That would be an ideal job for her that would not need supervision."

"I agree. What about Lady Aurelia?"

"She excels at investigating husbands and wives who have strayed from the home fires. We have several of those." She patted another pile of folders that was even higher than mine.

"And Mister Clapham?" A former Scotland Yard Detective Inspector who'd been our first hire. He was professional, thorough, and never failed to find his man . . . or woman.

"He's tracking down a witness for Sir Frederick. There's a reward if he finds him. He'll be gone for at least a week."

"What will you be working on?" I asked.

"We've been approached by Lady Hutton," Emma said in almost a whisper. "She's contemplating marriage again."

Twenty years ago, Sofia Campbell, a wealthy American heiress, had been sacrificed to her mother's ambitions, who yearned for a title for her daughter. Never mind Lord Hutton was in his fifties, a vicious drunk, and an avid gambler who'd lost most of his fortune at the gaming tables. While he gained a pile of money and a nubile, young wife on whom he could sire a son, she would become a marchioness. I doubted Miss Campbell had seen it as an advantageous marriage. Rumor had it, she'd cried during the entire wedding ceremony.

Regardless of her feelings on the matter, Lady Hutton had acted with distinction, giving Lord Hutton an heir and a spare. Rumor had it once that duty was done, she'd locked her bedroom door to him.

Over the passing years, Lord Hutton had grown even more dissolute. Not surprisingly, his health had suffered. Last year, he'd finally succumbed to his profligate ways. No one had mourned him, most especially Lady Hutton. But now it seemed she wanted to wed again.

"Does she want us to conduct a background check on the prospective groom?"

"No. It's the estate manager. She's known him for the last twenty years."

"So what would she like us to do?"

"She provided Lord Hutton with two sons. The older one inherited the title and the estate."

"I sense there's a fly in the ointment."

"There is. Lord Hutton's nephew was the presumptive heir until Lady Hutton provided her husband with a son."

"And a spare."

Lady Emma nodded. "The nephew claims that neither of her sons was sired by Lord Hutton. According to the nephew, he was unable to, er, perform."

"He wouldn't have a chance of proving the sons are illegitimate. According to the law, a husband is deemed the father when a child is born of his wife."

"True, but Lady Hutton doesn't believe that's the nephew's goal."

I pondered on that statement for a few seconds. "He wants to stain her reputation."

"Yes. But it wouldn't stop there. If the rumors gain purchase among the nobility, her sons' honor would suffer as well."

"I suppose the nephew is claiming the estate manager is the children's father?"

Emma offered a small smile. "You're nothing if not bright, Kitty."

"Does the nephew have any proof of this?"

"He claims he caught Lady Hutton and the estate manager in the greenhouse several times. *In flagrante delicto*, if you can believe it. They were so consumed with each other's they didn't notice him."

"And he never told his uncle?"

"Apparently not. He feared his allowance would be cut off. Meager as it was, he would have starved without it."

"And now I suppose he's blackmailing Lady Hutton."

"Yes. If she doesn't pay him, he'll spread the vile rumor among the nobility. There are those who would not only believe him but disseminate that juicy tidbit far and wide, especially the ladies who'd hoped to become Lady Hutton. She gained the prize they failed to win."

"Marriage to that man had to have been perfectly horrid."

"I agree. But some women would have put up with it all for the privilege of becoming a marchioness."

I shook my head. "I will never understand such ambition."

"They envy you too. And will me, once I become Lady Marlowe."

I squeezed her hand. "Good thing we both love our gentlemen."

Her cheeks flushed. "They are rather darling."

"Even when they're being impossible?"

"Even then." She shook her head and got back to business. "So, what do you think? Shall we take on the enquiry?"

Before I answered that question, I needed to know, "What exactly does Lady Hutton expect from us?"

"She wants us to investigate the nephew. She suspects he's just as reprehensible as his uncle. Once she has that proof, she can withhold his allowance. Apparently, it was written into Lord Hutton's will that the nephew must lead a blameless life if he wants to continue to receive it." She glanced off into the distance. "It'll be hard to prove, though."

"Why?"

"He's a vicar."

I burst out laughing. "You do have your work cut out for you."

"So we should take the enquiry?"

"Absolutely."

"I will have to travel to Oxfordshire. That's where his living is. Banbury, to be exact. It will take at least a week. Can you manage without me?"

"Absolutely. You should bring Marlowe along."

She feigned a rather scandalous expression. "Now, Kitty, what would our friends think?"

"That you're enjoying yourself?" She and Lord Marlowe were to be married in the fall. Although I doubted they would engage in intimate relations, tongues would most definitely wag if they were caught gallivanting around Oxfordshire on their own.

We both laughed once again.

Just as we were finishing our discussion, a knock sounded on her door. After Emma said, "Come in", Betsy, the agency's former receptionist and now full-time bookkeeper, peeked in. "I hope I'm not disturbing."

Emma and I both grinned. "We were just about done."

Practically vibrating with excitement, Betsy skipped into the office. "I have news to share. Neville and I have set our wedding date for the end of summer. Hopefully, by then, the agency won't be too busy?" I could hear the anxiety in her voice. "If that doesn't suit, we can change the date."

Emma and I immediately rose from our seats to embrace her, sharing in her joy and excitement.

"Wonderful news, Betsy!" I said warmly. "We must start planning at once!"

As we toasted to her upcoming nuptials with cups of Earl Grey, I couldn't help but think that while life continued at a brisk pace with mysteries to solve and responsibilities to shoulder, moments like these were what truly made it worthwhile.

CHAPTER 3

A LECTURE TO DIE FOR

The British Museum's lecture hall hummed with quiet anticipation as the Worthington family and Lily, Ned's fiancée, took our seats among a crowd eager to hear Richard speak. I'd hoped Robert would have been able to join us, but complications had arisen at the castle and brewery. So, unfortunately, his return had been delayed.

A set of ten lectures had been agreed upon between Richard and the museum with a different topic offered each Friday evening for the next two and a half months. Today's presentation would introduce the work of an Egyptian archaeologist to the audience. Subsequent ones would expound on Richard's individual excavations. The one most highly anticipated would focus on the opening of King Tut's tomb. After the British Museum announced the program of lectures, we'd expected some interest. But nothing prepared us for the crowd that had shown up.

"Oh, my!" Mother exclaimed. "It appears to be well attended."

"It's standing room only," Lily exclaimed. "Isn't it exciting?"

"Indeed, it is," Ned agreed.

Wearing a proud expression, Father said, "Richard should be pleased."

"I should say so," I said.

Our seats had been reserved at the front, cordoned off with a rope. Not only would we have the best view, but our presence would hopefully provide Richard with encouragement, if indeed any was needed.

Promptly at eight, a gong was struck three times. With each strike, the hall grew increasingly quieter. By the third one, it had grown silent. A gentleman I recognized as the British Museum director climbed the steps of the rectangular dais situated at the front of the hall and stepped up to the podium.

"Good evening, ladies and gentlemen. I'd like to welcome you to the first lecture of our program—*From Shifting Dunes to Sacred Tombs: The Art and Science of Egyptian Excavations.*"

A rather wordy title. But it had drawn a large crowd. So, who was I to judge?

"We have been fortunate to partner with noted archaeologist, Richard Worthington. His work on Egyptian excavations for the last several years has yielded several exciting finds. He will share with you his work in the Qau el-Kebir site. This archaeological concession is situated on the edge of the Eastern Desert, bordering the Nile's eastern floodplain. Now, without further ado, let us welcome our illustrious lecturer, Richard Worthington." As he finished speaking, he enthusiastically clapped, an action which was roundly seconded by those present.

As my brother stepped onto the dais, the hall illumination dimmed while a bright light focused solely on Richard. Behind him, seemingly out of thin air, a tableau materialized. A screen with a painted background of an Egyptian dig with pyramids and Egyptian structures in the background. Two laborers carrying chisels and trowels situated themselves next to the rocks that were placed in front of the painted screen.

As they moved into place, Richard began to speak. "Even though it was mid morn, the desert sun beat down upon us, unrelenting in its intensity." One of the laborers wiped his brow with a grimy handkerchief. "My shirt clung to my back, damp with sweat, and dust coated my boots, my trousers, even the folds of my sleeves." Putting action to words, he swept a hand across a sleeve, and dust cascaded to the ground. "Yet I hardly noticed. My eyes were fixed on the narrow trench before me, where two laborers were carefully brushing away layers of sand and stone. Every stroke of the brush seemed to breathe new life into the past."

As Richard spoke, the hall grew silent, the audience riveted on his every word.

"It had been months of grueling work. The excavation director kept us working day after day, convinced that we were close to something remarkable. Some of the men muttered their doubts in the evenings, claiming we were chasing a ghost. But I trusted our director. He had a sense for these things—an instinct honed through years of careful excavation and dogged persistence."

"Today had begun like any other. The morning air had been cool, almost pleasant, before the rising sun turned the plain into an oven. As the sun rose in the sky, my clothing became increasingly unbearable."

Richard had chosen to dress in what he termed his 'uniform'. A wide-brimmed hat, headscarf, vest, long-sleeved shirt, trousers, boots, gloves, a leather belt, and a satchel which he now shed. In dramatic fashion, he removed his hat and used the headscarf to wipe the perspiration from his face.

Even though the temperature in the room was temperate, his actions were such that I actually felt the heat. Such was the power of his suggestion.

"Suddenly, a laborer cried out. He'd found something. One of my many duties was to catalog whatever was discovered no matter how minute. I was also responsible for tracking our digging process and organizing the endless notes that piled up by the hour. I rushed over to examine what he'd found. After retrieving a brush from my belt—" he mimicked the motion "—I brushed away the debris of what turned out to be the fragment of a cup. I catalogued it in my notebook and handed it to our conservator."

For the next twenty minutes, he proceeded to put action to words as the laborers discovered more objects. Piece by piece, more of his garments came off until he was standing in only his shirt, trousers and belt. Finally, he took a flask from his belt and drank what I could only assume was water. When a stream of it dribbled down his neck into his now open shirt which showed bare flesh for anyone close enough to see, he employed the headscarf to wipe the moisture away. A round of decidedly feminine oohhhs circled the room.

Good heavens! Who knew Richard had that in him?

After another half hour of his demonstration, the laborers disappeared, and the lighting in the hall returned to normal. Stepping to the front of the dais, Richard said, "And thus at the end of our day, we bid goodnight and seek our well-earned rest." With a no doubt well-rehearsed flourish, he bowed.

One and all the audience came to their feet with thunderous applause.

The director of the British Museum, appearing somewhat

astonished, stepped up to the dais. Gazing at Richard, he said, "That was rather, er, illuminating, Mister Worthington, but wonderful indeed." He turned back to the audience. "Mister Worthington's next lecture will be a week from tonight. As this event has stirred such a strong interest, a ticket will be required to attend. So, plan accordingly."

Rather than remain, Richard rushed out the hall side door. Good thing too, for he would have been mobbed.

As it turned out, he didn't entirely disappear. A champagne reception was being held in a private room of the British Museum for the more illustrious patrons. We'd barely arrived there when Richard strolled into the space. He'd changed into proper gentleman's wear. As soon as he entered the room, he was surrounded by highly excited ladies.

I glanced at Ned, who was fighting back a grin.

"That was a rather, er, interesting lecture," Mother said somewhat hesitantly.

"I think it was marvelous," I said. "If he'd stood up there talking for an hour about what he did, the audience would have been bored to tears. Instead, he demonstrated it in dramatic fashion. The audience was riveted."

"Especially members of the fairer sex," Ned said, calmly sipping his champagne.

Lily laughed. "Yes, indeed."

"Did he always have that in him?" I asked no one in particular.

"Young women of quality were always buzzing around him," Mother said. "Of course, that did not last long. When the Great War broke out, he enlisted. And after that, he began his excavation work in Egypt."

Sometime later, Richard freed himself from his adoring fans and joined us. "What did you think?"

"You were wonderful, darling," Mother said.

"You had everyone riveted," I offered.

"Great job, son," Father patted him on the back. "What did the director say?"

"He's turning people away," Richard said with a grin. "There are only so many tickets to be had. He wants me to do more lectures. But . . . I'd like to explore other endeavors."

Mother's expression grew fearful. "Hopefully none that would take you away from England."

Richard curled an arm around her shoulders. "Don't worry, Mother. I aim to stay put. But there's a whole array of things I could do. Archaeology is not just about excavating the past but also preserving it and sharing its stories with the world. He paused for a moment. "I seem to have an aptitude for getting people's attention."

"Especially those from the distaff side," Ned murmured, firmly tongue in cheek.

Richard laughed. "Yes, I noticed that." He nodded to some who were sending come-hither glances his way.

"No wonder," I said. "Admit it, Richard. You're a catch."

He blushed. "Can we change the subject, please?"

"Of course," I said. It was the truth, though. Not only was he handsome but he had a quite attractive physique. Thankfully, after his bout with malaria, he'd gained back most of his weight. He was also quite intelligent, and, thanks to Father, possessed a nice fortune.

"Why don't you give us a tour of the Egyptian exhibit?" Mother asked. "I've never seen it."

"Of course." He crooked an arm to her, and together they walked out of the room with us in tow. I paid little attention to the artifacts he pointed out as my mind was on Robert. Little did I know how important the Egyptian exhibit would become in the days ahead.

CHAPTER 4

A DAUGHTER LOST

*A*s I followed the butler, I couldn't help but be impressed by the Mayfair Fallon residence. The grandeur of the Georgian period veritably seeped from its very walls.

While the architecture boasted high ceilings and intricate plasterwork, portraits of ancestors dating back to Charles II adorned the sides of the space. Each portrait was a testament to the wealth and style of that era. The men depicted in long wigs and sash stockings, their feet, encased in polished buckled shoes, gleamed almost as much as the gilded frames that housed their likenesses. The ladies wore bell-shaped skirts and pagoda sleeves, their high heels and lace trimmings on their gowns adding a delicate yet elaborate touch to their opulent attire. Impressive indeed.

I entered the drawing room expecting to find Lady Fallon, but to my surprise, she was not there.

"I will inform Lady Fallon of your arrival," the very prim and proper butler declared in a firm tone. "She wishes you to make yourself at home."

"Thank you." Rather than sit, I opted to wander around the room.

The furniture around me was heavy and ornate, with thick, luxurious fabrics and cushions that hinted at the no-expense-spared attitude that must have governed their selection. Everything was gilded, reflecting the soft light of the chandeliers in a way that bathed the room in a warm, golden glow.

A portrait of an older gentleman who appeared to be in his sixties hung over a bombe chest. White haired and brown eyed, his no-nonsense gaze seemed to challenge me. Probably wondering what my purpose was.

Suddenly, the door swung open, and what I can only describe as a vision of refined elegance and silent strength glided into the room. Her skin was like porcelain, flawless and smooth, giving her an almost ethereal quality that was accentuated by her choice of attire—a stunning bias-cut dress more than likely created by the French designer Madeleine Vionnet. The fabric flowed around her with every movement, the innovative cut enhancing her delicate figure and lending her an air of fragile vulnerability that the heavy, structured garments of her husband's ancestors could never have achieved.

"Miss Worthington, or shall I say Lady Rutledge, thank you for coming to my aid," she said, coming forward.

Wouldn't you know it? Her voice matched her appearance. "Either is fine. And I'm more than happy to help."

"Won't you take a seat?" She pointed to a sofa upholstered in a dark blue brocade. "I've ordered tea as well as coffee. I understand you prefer the latter."

"Thank you," I said, accommodating myself on the furnishing. She did likewise on the matching one facing mine. A small table rested between us.

We had no opportunity to engage in conversation as the door opened once more to admit a footman and a maid carrying not only a tray with the tea and coffee service but another one filled with all kinds of delicate pastries.

While she poured our chosen beverages and plated two pastries each, I couldn't help but draw parallels between her and the ancestral portraits lining the walls of her grand Mayfair mansion.

Although dressed in the height of 1920s fashion, her beauty and style could easily have placed her among the courtiers of Charles II's era without a second glance. But her blonde hair styled in a modern bob was a stark contrast to the elaborate arrangements of those long-ago Fallon ancestors. Her dark blue eyes seemed to hold stories of both joy and sorrow, reflecting a depth that was both alluring and poignant.

Once we'd duly sipped our tea and coffee and shared the polite pleasantries that etiquette demanded, I fetched a notebook and a pen from the satchel I'd brought with me. It was time to question her. "Tell me about Miranda."

That polite facade she'd so carefully constructed collapsed in an instant. "She's embroiled herself in this . . . cult. I don't know what to do." As she spoke, her cup trembled in the saucer, so much so I was afraid the tea would spill over.

Reaching over, I stilled her shaky hand. "We will arrive at that point later. But for now, tell me about her. What does she like to do? Dance? Read? Play the piano? Begin with that."

Her shoulders relaxed as the tension left her. "She was rather lovely growing up. But then a mother would always say that about her child." A sad sort of chuckle escaped her.

"My mother was dead honest about her children. She knew what trouble we were, especially me. Although she'd never admit it in public."

A soft smile bloomed across her mouth. "How very fortunate you were."

"Still am. Now tell me what Miranda likes to do."

Rather than answer, she came to her feet and took to wandering about the room, finally settling next to a window overlooking her glorious garden. "She loved nature when she was younger. Whenever she went missing, I would always find her playing in the dirt."

"She didn't go away to school?"

Lady Fallon veered sharply toward me. "No. I could never bear to part from her."

"Neither did my mother. My sisters and I were educated at home."

Her brow furrowed. "Sisters? I thought you only had one, the Duchess of Wynchcombe." She was well-versed on our family.

"There were three of us. Margaret, Emily and I. Sadly, Emily succumbed to the Spanish flu."

Her eyes softened with sympathy. "I'm so very sorry."

"Thank you." I allowed a few seconds to elapse before asking, "What did Miranda hope for her future? Did she envision marriage and children or something else?"

She waved a hand in the air, a gesture of sorts. "We never really talked about it. I thought she would enjoy her debut season, find a nice young man to marry, and have babies. She never asked, and I didn't mention it. It was just what was expected, you see."

"I understand." That would be Miranda's path, especially with her family history. But something had changed.

She must have sensed my unspoken question because she rushed to assert. "We were happy, Miss Worthington.

Tolbert, Miranda, and I." She glanced at the painting of the older man. "He was such a kind man. There was a twenty-year difference between us, but I loved him dearly. And he loved me. He loved us. We were never far away from each other. Even when Tolbert had to travel for business, he took us with him. He never wanted to be separated from us."

Her emotions seemed to overwhelm her, and she stopped speaking for several moments. But then, all her pain poured out. "And then one day, he was gone. His heart gave out." She turned away once more, probably to hide her tears.

"I'm so sorry."

She veered back towards me. "Thank you. We were devastated, Miranda and I. We should have found solace in each other. Instead, we grew apart. That's when she started to change."

"In what way?"

She took her seat on the sofa once more. "She wanted to know why her father had been so cruelly taken from her. They had a special relationship, you see. Much closer than most fathers and daughters. Tolbert relished her bright mind, her sharp inquisitiveness. He was so very proud of her. When he . . . died, it all disappeared. I tried. Heaven knows I tried to praise her efforts, congratulate her on her accomplishments. But it wasn't the same. I could never take his place."

"You provided your own strength and support as her mother."

"Yes, I did."

"So, what did Miranda do?"

"She desperately searched for answers. In books at first. And then she turned to religion. We're Church of England. Always have been. But she was not able to find what she sought there. Eager to divert her thoughts, I arranged for us to travel. Italy, Spain, Greece. But none of it helped. As we explored other lands, other cultures, she grew even more restless." When she spoke of Miranda, her voice trembled, betraying the fear and despair she was working so hard to mask.

"And then one day, almost out of the blue," Lady Fallon continued, "Miranda expressed a wish to visit Egypt. We were in Athens at the time, so Egypt was not so very far. I arranged for a sailing ship to take us to Alexandria. From there, we made our way to Cairo and then Giza to see the Sphinx and the pyramids. She was fascinated by them, couldn't get enough. For the first time in a long while, I saw her smile. You can't imagine the joy I felt. But that happiness did not last long. Three days into our visit, she went missing. I was frantic. I thought she'd been kidnapped, you see. She wasn't. She'd gone on her own volition to the Temple of Osiris. Do you know who that is?"

"I can't say that I do."

"In ancient Egyptian mythology, Osiris was the god of the underworld, fertility, agriculture, and resurrection."

"Ah," I said.

"You can see where that fits in."

"She wanted her father to be brought back to life."

"Yes. We left the very next day, came straight back to London. As it turned out, it was not far enough. Somehow, some way, she found her way to a group calling themselves the Cult of Osiris, based right here in London." Her hands fluttered like caged birds while she expressed her worries about her daughter's involvement with the mysterious Egyptian cult.

I would have been as well.

"Miss Worthington, I am quite desperate," Lady Fallon admitted, her voice a mix of the refined and the frantic as she sat opposite me. "They've filled her head with notions of

Egyptian gods and promises of eternal life. I fear something truly awful will happen to her."

Her fear was not unfounded. A cult that believed in resurrection may very well put that belief to the test, with Miranda being the sacrificial lamb. In ancient times, when the earth lay fallow in the winter only to be reborn in the spring, it made sense to believe in such a deity. But to apply that same belief now was illogical at best, and downright lunacy at worst. Human beings could not be resurrected. But blind faith never questioned its gods. It simply believed. If I were to find Miranda, I would need more information. "When did Miranda leave, Lady Fallon?"

"Three weeks ago," she replied, her voice faltering slightly. "She left a note saying she had found what she needed with this cult. I've tried everything to locate her. Discreetly, of course. Her presentation to their majesties and her coming-out ball are happening in less than a month. A scandal could be disastrous."

"Understandable," I murmured, noting the urgency of the situation. "Was there anything else in her note, or anything she mentioned that could lead us to her?"

"Only that she met an Egyptian woman named Isis at the museum's Egyptian exhibition."

"Did Miranda visit the museum on her own?"

"No. Before we left on our travels, I hired a woman, Miss Fletcher, to escort my daughter during those times I was unable to do so. Although Miss Fletcher had nothing to do with Miranda's visit to the Temple of Osiris in Egypt, she did accompany her to the British Museum. If I'd known about those excursions, I would have forbidden them."

"Miss Fletcher didn't tell you where they were going?"

"No." She hitched up her chin. "That's why I terminated her employment. Without a reference, I might add."

Rather unfortunate, as I would need to talk to Miss

Fletcher. "Do you have a forwarding address? I'd like to question her."

"I hired her through an agency—The Genteel Companions Guild. She came highly recommended." A pause later, she added, "I realize now I shouldn't have let her go. But I was so angry at her."

"Understandably so. I'll contact the Companions Guild. They should be able to provide me with her address." I jotted that information in my notebook. "Museums are public places. Someone there might recall seeing Miranda. Do you have a likeness of her? It would help to have that."

"Yes, of course." She strolled toward a small table at the far end of the room where several miniatures rested. After choosing one, she brought it back to me. "This was painted two years ago, when she turned fifteen. It's a very good likeness."

"She's quite beautiful," I said. Miranda's wide, luminous brown eyes held a quiet intensity, and her chestnut hair—thick and glossy as polished mahogany—framed her face in gentle waves. There was a clear resemblance to her father, more than her mother; perhaps his hair, in his youth, had gleamed with that same warm hue.

"Thank you."

"I understand she's seventeen."

She nodded. "Her eighteenth is but a few days from now."

"What about her friends? Anyone who might share her interests or who might have joined her?"

"Before I terminated her employment, Miss Fletcher mentioned a young man, Julian Banks from Oxford, whom Miranda met at the museum. Apparently, he shared Miranda's fascination with Egyptology. But there was no mention of him in her note."

I wrote down his name. "I'll do my best to locate Mister Banks and speak with him." Richard would know someone I could contact in Oxford, and maybe someone at the museum knew who he was. "Sometimes the most unlikely threads lead us to the truth." Standing, I reassured her, "I'll do everything in my power to bring Miranda back to you."

Her smile was shaky, but sincere as she came to her feet. "Thank you, Miss Worthington. You truly are my last hope."

CHAPTER 5

A DISCUSSION WITH RICHARD

Upon my return home, I wasted no time telephoning Richard. As it turned out, he was at the British Museum preparing for his next lecture. We arranged to meet at three, which would give me enough time to bathe and change into one of my usual business dresses. The haute couture gown I'd worn to Lady Fallon's would not do at the museum.

An hour later, I strode into the building, my mind preoccupied with the complexities of my case. Today, I wasn't just visiting as a member of the public. I had a mission—to discuss the Cult of Osiris with Richard and to glean any connections he might have at Oxford that would lead me to Julian Banks. As I approached the information desk, a large banner caught my eye. It advertised Richard's upcoming lecture on mummification—a topic decidedly different from the one he'd been planning to discuss.

Slightly mystified about the change of topic, I approached the information desk. "Hello."

"How may I help you?" the docent asked with a friendly smile.

"My name is Kitty Worthington. I'm here to see my brother, Richard Worthington. He's expecting me."

The docent smiled brightly. "Oh, yes. He's expecting you." She came to her feet. "If you would please follow me, I will escort you to the hall."

"There's no need. I attended his first lecture. I know the way."

"Actually, there's been a change. The lectures have been moved to the Great Hall. It's the largest one in the museum," she whispered almost conspiratorially. "So many people have bought tickets, his entire series is sold out."

"How marvelous!" Richard had spent a great deal of time on his presentations. I was glad they'd drawn so much interest.

"Yes, indeed. I managed to obtain two tickets. Can't wait to hear the one on mummification. He's going to do a demonstration."

"On a real body?" I asked with a laugh.

The receptionist looked horrified. "Heavens, no!"

"I was joking."

"Yes, of course." Still she looked askance at me.

Finally, after walking down numerous corridors, we reached the Great Hall.

"Here we are," the docent said.

"Thank you. You've been very helpful. I can take it from here."

"Of course."

As I entered the massive hall, I couldn't help but be impressed. It was easily three times the size of the previous one. This one seemed to hold over three hundred seats, where the one I'd attended before had held only around one hundred.

I spotted Richard at the far end of the hall, deep in conversation with an assistant who was setting up several jars and odd-looking instruments on a wide bench located in the back of the dais. The long table positioned in the front more than likely would be reserved for the 'mummy.'

When I was within a few feet, Richard caught sight of me. He quickly excused himself and greeted me with a warm, brotherly hug.

"It's good to see you, Kitty."

"Likewise," I said, embracing him. "I hear your lectures have become quite popular."

"Can you believe it?" He appeared quite proud of himself. "They're sold out of all the lecture tickets."

"The docent mentioned it. Congratulations! I'm so happy for you."

"Thank you. It feels good to have my work recognized."

"I saw the banner announcing your next lecture at the reception desk. Why the change to mummification?"

"The museum director decided a more . . . sensational topic might attract more Elite patrons. He was right. The number of Elite patrons has tripled in the last week. That means more funds will be made available for educational programs at the museum."

"That's wonderful."

"Yes, it is. I'm glad I'm able to contribute to such a worthy cause." The assistant approached him with a question about a tool, which Richard readily answered before turning back to me. "So, you want to talk about the god Osiris?"

"Yes, it's for a case I'm working on."

"Let's take a seat in the back. We won't be overheard there."

"You're not tiring yourself, are you?" I asked after we

accommodated ourselves. It was a fair question. He'd just recuperated from a bout of malaria.

"No." When I arched a brow, he said, "Well, maybe a little. But all I need is a short rest. Our conversation should just about do it."

He was used to working long hours on his archaeological digs, but he'd been hale and hearty then. If he exhausted himself preparing for the lectures, he might suffer a relapse. "You might need more than that, Richard." He was looking a bit pale. "How much longer do you have here?"

"An hour, maybe two."

"Promise me no more than that."

"Very well. I promise," he said, grinning.

"What?" I asked.

"I always looked upon you as my little sister, and here you are all worried about me."

"We always worried about you, Richard, especially Mother. You just were not around to see it."

His smile faltered. "I should have come home more often."

"You are here now," I said, pressing his hand. "And we are all so very proud of you." I paused briefly before bringing up the subject I wished to discuss. "Now tell me about Osiris."

"He was one of the most important gods in ancient Egypt. He was seen as the god of fertility, agriculture, the afterlife, the dead, and resurrection. Indeed, life itself. A very powerful deity. Why are you interested in him?"

I shared the information I'd learned from Lady Fallon. "Do you know of a group called the Cult of Osiris? They're supposedly located here in London."

"Can't say that I do. But I know several individuals, experts in Egyptian culture and religion, who might. Do you want me to contact them?"

"Yes, please, but I'll need to talk to them myself. If they agree to do so, of course."

"I'd like to come along, if you don't mind. It might facilitate your discussions."

"You are more than welcome to do so. You would know better than me the right questions to ask." A sudden idea occurred to me. "Would Zubair be able to help?" Zubair had brought Richard back to us when my brother had succumbed to malaria. If he hadn't done so, Richard would more than likely have died.

"He would, if he were here. But he returned to Egypt. London grew too cold for him, and he missed his family. I was sad to see him go."

"I can imagine." Zubair had been Richard's assistant during the years my brother had been in Egypt. "Lady Fallon also mentioned a woman named Isis. Miranda apparently talked to her at least once. Does that name sound familiar?"

"No. But there's likely a connection between her and this cult. Isis was the sister-wife of the god Osiris."

"Sister-wife?"

He smiled. "It was not unusual for brothers and sisters to marry in ancient Egyptian culture."

"Heavens!"

"It helped preserve the dynasties. Of course, it also introduced abnormalities in their offspring."

"But how did he become such a powerful god?"

"As the god of agriculture, he was responsible for the death and rebirth of the crops. He himself supposedly died, murdered by his brother according to one theory. His body was placed in a coffin and tossed into the Nile River. His wife Isis found him and brought him back to life."

"That sort of makes sense."

"There is a bloodier version of his death and resurrection. After Isis found him, she cut him into several pieces and buried them throughout Egypt so the earth would be fertile again."

I shivered. "Let's move off that gruesome image for a moment. Lady Fallon mentioned that Miranda had met a Julian Banks who supposedly had a connection to Oxford."

"The name's not familiar. I could reach out to my former archaeology professors and see if they've heard of him."

"Thank you. I appreciate it."

Just then, the assistant approached Richard once more. This time, Richard introduced him. "Kitty, this is Mister Branson. He'll be assisting me with the presentation." He pointed to me. "And this is my sister, Catherine Worthington, er, Crawford Sinclair, Lady Rutledge."

I laughed. "Stop. Kitty Worthington will do."

"A pleasure to meet you, Miss Worthington."

I decided it was time to leave. I'd obtained as much information as I could. The rest would have to wait. But before I could say goodbye, Richard pointed to a vase Mister Branson was holding, "Where did you get this?"

"Dr. Henderson," Mister Branson said. "He had several pieces delivered. He thought they'd be of use for your lecture."

A highly perturbed Richard came to his feet. "Show me the other items."

With the assistant in tow, Richard ate up the space to the bench where the objects that the assistant had been working on rested.

Curiosity got the better of me, so I remained right where I was.

"This is wrong," Richard said, frowning.

"Is it not a proper vase, Mister Worthington?"

"It's a proper one, but it shouldn't be here."

Rather than ask the obvious question, the assistant remained silent. I didn't blame him. Richard had gone from perturbed to downright angry. Why couldn't the object be here? Was it because he did not wish it to be, or some other reason?

Before I could inquire about it, two gentlemen entered the hall, the sound of their sure steps echoing in the hall. One was the director of the museum. The other was unfamiliar. He had a slight paunch and greying, red hair that added a vivid splash of color to the somber colors of his apparel. His air of superiority seemed to demand respect.

"Ah, Lady Rutledge," the director said. "How wonderful to see you again. Have you met Martin Henderson, our Egyptian antiquities curator?"

"I have not had the pleasure. How do you do, Mister Henderson?"

"Doctor, actually. I earned my degree from Oxford."

"Ah, my apologies. I did not know."

"Lady Rutledge." Henderson lowered his head, usually a sign of respect. But the smirk on his lips indicated derision. A proud, disagreeable man to be sure. Addressing Richard, he said, "I see the artifacts were delivered. I thought you could use them during your mummification lecture."

"How did you obtain this piece?" Richard asked, pointing to the vase. Apparently, he was in no mood to be polite.

"I beg your pardon," Henderson said.

"This piece belongs to the Cairo Museum. It's an alabaster vase discovered in the tomb of Tutankhaman."

Henderson's haughty brow took a hike. "How could you possibly tell? After all, Egyptian alabaster vases are very similar."

"This one is different. It's adorned with stoppers sculpted as protective deities. I was awarded the privilege of holding it in my hands. It's quite unique."

"What are you claiming, Sir?"

"This vase was stolen from the Cairo Museum."

"How dare you imply such a thing? You impugn my honor."

The director of the museum rushed in to pour oil over the troubled waters. "Come, come, gentlemen. I'm sure there's a perfectly logical explanation." He turned to the red-haired gentleman, "Martin, could you please examine your records and identify how and from whom you obtained this vase. Then we can satisfy Mister Worthington's curiosity."

Henderson managed to rein in his anger long enough to say, "Very well." And then he stormed out of the hall.

The director tossed an arm around Richard, not an easy thing to do since he was several inches shorter. "Now, Mister Worthington, you've been working very hard on your lectures, something we truly appreciate. Why don't you cease your labors for the day, and we will pick it up tomorrow. By then Doctor Henderson should have the provenance of the canopic jar."

"Very well."

"That's the ticket." The director turned to face Richard's helpers, who'd been quietly watching the drama play out. "As a matter of fact, why don't you all cease work for the day?"

A chorus of "Yes, sirs" and "thank yous" echoed from the dais. Mister Branson, however, did not leave right away. Instead, he asked, "Shouldn't we pack everything before we leave?"

Before Richard could say anything, the director responded, "I'll get someone to do it. Just go." His voice carried a tone of impatience. Obviously, he didn't like his authority challenged.

"Yes, Sir." With one last concerned look at Richard, the assistant followed the other helpers out of the hall.

"I can help with the packing," Richard said. "In fact, I would prefer it."

"Why?" the director asked.

Richard took a measured breath before answering. "Some of the artifacts are very fragile. They need to be handled with care."

The director brushed a hand across his brow. "I know. We'll take good care of them, I promise. Just leave, Richard, please."

A clear dismissal. Putting on a bright smile, I curled my arm around Richard's. "Why don't we leave together? We can have a nice chat on the way home."

"Thank you, Lady Rutledge," the museum director said, appearing somewhat relieved. "Your assistance is much appreciated." He patted Richard on the back. "See you tomorrow, young man."

Almost by mutual consent, Richard and I maintained silence while he fetched his things. Outside the museum, it took no time to find a taxicab as a stream of visitors were disembarking from several. But once we were ensconced in the vehicle, I said, "Tell me about the vase."

"It came from King Tut's tomb. I would stake my reputation on it."

I wasn't about to challenge his belief. "How could it have ended at the British Museum?"

"Stolen obviously." The opening of King Tut's tomb had been a huge endeavor. It had first been discovered three years ago, but the cataloguing and removal of all the objects found within were still going on. Since the tomb was in Egypt, the artifacts belonged to the Cairo Museum. Or at least they should have been.

"Wouldn't you have heard about it?"

"Not necessarily. The Cairo Museum wouldn't want it known that a precious antiquity from King Tut's tomb has gone missing."

We arrived at Worthington House in no time at all. So, unfortunately, more of my questions would have to wait. I would see him tomorrow at his next lecture, so I simply said goodnight and suggested he get some rest. I doubted he would. More than likely, he would spend the evening consumed with thoughts over what he'd discovered. Unless his suspicions were allayed tomorrow at the museum, fireworks were likely to erupt.

CHAPTER 6

A PUBLIC CONFRONTATION

*T*he following morning, I was savoring a second cup of coffee before heading to the detective agency. With Emma off to Oxfordshire on the Lady Hudson matter, it was up to me to manage things. But before I could do so, the trill of the telephone punctured the quiet of my parlor. Hoping it was Robert, I eagerly picked up the receiver. "Hello."

"Kitty? It's Richard."

"Oh, good morning." I couldn't help but be disappointed. Robert called every morning around this time. And then another thought occurred to me. "Is everything all right?"

"Better than alright. Rather than sit around stewing over things, I called my old Oxford professor to inquire about Julian Banks. Turns out, he knows him quite well."

The news sparked a flutter of hope in my chest. "Marvelous. What did he say?"

"He was very complimentary. Julian was quite the scholar,

particularly fascinated with Egyptology and eager to get involved in an excavation project in Egypt. My professor provided him with the names of several individuals in London as well as letters of introduction."

"That sounds promising. Did he give you Julian's address?"

"He did, as well as his telephone number. As it turns out, Julian had been traveling to Italy and Greece and just returned to London about two months ago. Do you have paper and pen?"

"Absolutely." I grabbed my notebook and jotted down the information he gave me, including Julian Banks's phone number. "Thank you, Richard. This is more than I hoped for."

We exchanged a few more pleasantries before I set down the receiver. I would need to telephone Julian Banks and make an appointment to talk to him. But before doing so, I needed to jot down the questions I needed answered. Thankfully, Julian Banks was at his address, and he agreed to meet at one. That would give me enough time to stop at the agency and see if there were any pressing issues that needed to be handled.

Thankfully, no urgent matters had surfaced. Although two new clients had need of our services, Amelia had taken them on as they were minor at best. So, at thirty past twelve, I found myself navigating the bustling streets of London to Julian Banks' address. His townhouse was situated in a respectable leafy neighborhood on a quiet street, far removed from the chaos of the city center. As I approached the polished oak door, my reflections on what questions to prioritize were interrupted by the door swinging open.

"Miss Worthington?"

"Yes."

"So happy to meet you," he held out his hand and pumped mine with great enthusiasm.

The man who stood before me was a far cry from the moth-eaten academics who usually inhabited Oxford, but then he was not a professor, but a recent graduate. Julian Banks was young, perhaps in his mid twenties, with sharp blue eyes and dark hair that fell in a stylish tousle over his brow. He was dressed impeccably in a dark suit that spoke of a man used to the finer things in life, not just dusty tombs and ancient relics.

"As you've probably guessed, I'm Julian Banks." His voice was warm, his smile inviting. "Please, come in."

"Thank you, Mister Banks. I appreciate you seeing me on such short notice," I said, stepping into the foyer, which was as tastefully appointed as its owner.

"Not at all, and please call me Julian. Can't tell you how thrilled I am to meet Richard Worthington's sister."

"Ah." No wonder he was so excited. He wanted to work at an excavation in Egypt. My brother had done so for the last several years. More than likely, he envisioned an introduction to, and maybe a recommendation from, my illustrious brother.

"You said on the telephone you wanted to know about my conversations with Lady Miranda?"

"Yes."

"Why don't we proceed to the drawing room. We can talk there. I've arranged for coffee and tea."

"How very splendid of you."

Once we arrived there, I glanced around the exquisitely decorated space. "What a gorgeous room."

"Thank you, but I can't take credit for it. It's my parents' house. They're on a sea voyage to South America at the moment. Father has interests in Argentina. He's particularly worried about its political climate. Anarchists and communists are threatening to overthrow the social order. He's hoping to salvage what he can."

"I wish him luck then."

"Thank you."

Our conversation was interrupted by a maid who entered with the tea and coffee service. After asking permission to play Mother, I poured cups for us both.

After taking a sip of the brew, Julian asked, "So what in particular do you wish me to tell you about Lady Miranda?"

"Everything about your encounters."

He frowned. "I haven't seen her lately at the museum. Has something happened to her?"

Lady Fallon had not given me permission to share the news about Miranda's disappearance. So, all I could say was, "Her mother wishes to know more about your friendship with her, that's all. Miranda is only seventeen, you see, and she worries."

His brow cleared up. "Understandably so. Well, let's see. There isn't much to tell. I only saw her twice. The first time was about two months ago. Right around Christmas."

Odd time of year to visit a museum when there were so many other jolly things to do in London during the holiday. But to each his own.

"Were both times at the British Museum?"

"Yes. Sorry. I should have said. I was studying the wooden coffin of Pasenhor, an influential member of the Libyan Meshwesh tribe. They settled in Egypt during the 22nd Dynasty—around 725 BC. His wooden coffin is decorated with religious scenes and spells from the Book of the Dead."

I couldn't help but be impressed. "You know your Egyptian history."

"I've always been fascinated by it."

"Was Lady Miranda as enthralled?"

"She was. She had traveled to Egypt with her mother and was fortunate enough to see the pyramids and the Sphinx. I had as well, so we compared notes. I was struck by how knowledgeable she was."

"Did you part as friends?"

His brow wrinkled. "More like acquaintances. Her chaperone stood over her the entire time. As you can imagine, her presence did not encourage a close friendship."

"No indeed. When did you see her again?"

He glanced off into the distance as if he were trying to remember. "Two weeks later, I believe. She'd changed."

"How so?"

"She seemed more . . . worldly. As it was just about lunchtime, she suggested a visit to a tea shoppe close to the museum where we could satisfy our appetites. We had quite an extensive discussion. As I recall, she was particularly fascinated by the god Osiris."

That tracked with what Lady Fallon had said.

"When she asked me if I believed in resurrection, I sensed there was more to her question than a scholarly discussion. Our luncheon ended shortly after that, as I had an afternoon appointment. That's the last time I saw her."

"Did she mention someone named Isis?"

"As in the wife of Osiris?"

"No. This would be a person she supposedly met."

"I don't recall her mentioning such a name." His brow knitted once more. "Surely her chaperone would know."

"Unfortunately, she's no longer in the employ of Lady Fallon."

His expression changed subtly as a shadow passed over his features. "Forgive me for saying so, but these questions seem to stem from more than a mother's concern. Has something happened to Lady Miranda?" he asked again.

I sensed no darkness in him, no double-dealing. Lady Fallon may not have given me permission to share the details regarding Miranda, but I felt that I could trust him. More than that, he could become an ally. "She abandoned her home. Her mother doesn't know where she is."

His eyes grew wide. "Truly?"

"Afraid so. Lady Fallon hired me to find her. She said she'd joined the Cult of Osiris. Have you heard of it?"

"No. But I know someone who might. My Oxford professor provided me with letters of introduction to a noted Egyptian scholar. We've already held a discussion. I can reach out to him if you wish."

"I'd like to talk to him myself."

"Yes, of course. I'll telephone him this afternoon. How should I explain things?"

"Tell him I'm trying to locate a missing young woman who may have gotten herself involved in an Egyptian cult. Just don't reveal Lady Miranda's name."

"No, of course not."

Having achieved what I could, I came to my feet. "Thank you, Julian, you've been very helpful."

"You're most welcome." He paused for a moment before asking the question which must have been uppermost in his mind. "May I ask a favor of you?"

"An introduction to my brother, Richard?"

"Am I so transparent?" he asked with a lopsided grin.

"No. I'd be more than glad to arrange a meeting. As a matter of fact, he's holding another lecture tonight."

He appeared crestfallen. "I know. I tried to get tickets, but they were sold out."

"I'm sure we can arrange one for you. Our entire Worthington family is planning to attend. Meet us by the information desk. Say half past seven?"

"I'll be there. Thank you, Miss Worthington."

"Thank you for your time. You've given me much to consider."

"It was my pleasure. And please, if there's anything else you need, don't hesitate to ask."

Stepping out of the house, I felt a mix of elation and trepidation. I'd made progress. Not much, some. Still, it was movement in the right direction. I had a good feeling about Julian. He reminded me of a younger Richard. Hopefully, he would prove to be an ally. Only time would tell.

CHAPTER 7

TURMOIL AT THE BRITISH MUSEUM

I arrived home hoping Robert had telephoned. It was unlike him to go an entire day without contacting me. As I started to hand my outer garments to our butler, my first question was, "Have we heard from Lord Rutledge?"

Rather than answer, Mister Black fought back a smile. Strange. Our butler hardly ever demonstrated that emotion.

"He certainly has," a voice cried out from the library entrance.

"Robert!" I flew toward him, dragging my coat behind me. "You're home."

"Indeed, I am, darling."

Closing the library door behind us, he tossed my coat on a chair and took me into his arms. We kissed, deeply, passionately. "I missed you," he said once we'd come up for air.

I curled my arms around him. "Not as much as I missed you. But how did you manage to get away?" Yesterday, he'd mentioned he would need to remain at Chipping Bliss a few more days.

"It was made clear that my presence was no longer needed. Indeed, I was encouraged to return to London."

"Who dared say such a thing?" Not that I was surprised. Sometimes his thoroughness tended to grate people's nerves.

"The estate, distillery, and brewery managers. They explained that, while they fully appreciated my assistance, they could manage from there."

Laughter escaped me. "Oh, Robert."

He returned my embrace with a gentle strength. "How has everything been here?"

"There's quite a bit to tell you," I began, my mind racing with the day's events. After we settled into our usual spot in the library, I recounted everything that had transpired at the British Museum, leaving nothing out.

Robert's brow furrowed in thought. "It sounds serious," he noted, his tone laced with concern. "I was going to suggest an early evening, but clearly we must attend Richard's lecture."

His understanding was just another reason I loved him so deeply. "Yes, we do need to be there. Something is unfolding, and it's not quite clear yet how it will all play out."

After an early supper, we set out for the museum. The evening was crisp, the sky a clear vault speckled with stars as we made our way through the bustling streets of London.

Julian Banks was exactly where I'd asked him to be. After explaining to the docent that he was part of the Worthington family, a ticket for Richard's lecture was located for him.

When we arrived at the great hall, it was already teeming with people. Mostly seated, but a fair amount were standing as every seat had been filled. Excited chatter filled the space, no doubt with anticipation and scholarly curiosity. In one corner of the room, a group of rather earnest-looking enthusiasts had gathered, many clutching notebooks or pamphlets like holy writ. One of them recognized Julian as he waved and called out his name.

"You know him?"

"Oh, yes. We took lectures together at Oxford. A rather fervent chap."

I would need to get his details from Julian. Maybe he'd met Miranda.

My family was already seated prominently in the front row. I had not had the chance to discuss the day's developments with them, but apparently Richard had briefed them on the essentials as Mother whispered, "I know." After a quick introduction to Julian, we took our seats. There was no time for more as the lights suddenly dimmed, leaving only the podium illuminated.

The director of the museum introduced Richard with his usual fanfare, and the lighting dimmed as Richard took the stage. When he reached the center, the lights snapped back on. And there he stood, dressed in the elaborate robes of an Egyptian priest, standing next to the table I'd seen before. With dramatic fanfare, he unveiled the mummified body. Some in the audience screamed, many gasped. Chatter spread as people commented on what they were seeing, mostly along the lines of "Is that real?" Of course, it wasn't. Richard had crafted it out of cloth, wires, resin, ashes, clay, and tea he'd used to stain the linen. But it appeared real enough to make anyone shiver. He was a showman, my brother.

"Ladies and gentlemen," he began, his voice clear and commanding despite the soft echo of the room, "today we shall delve into the fascinating, intricate world of ancient Egyptian mummification."

Although I'd heard Richard rattle off facts about sarcophagi and burial rites often enough, something about seeing him in his element, surrounded by scrolls and spotlights, made the topic more enthralling.

"The process began with purification," Richard continued. "The body of the deceased was washed with palm wine," he said as an assistant handed him a container, "and then rinsed with water from the Nile." Another vessel was passed to him. "A sacred river to the Egyptians. This was not merely hygienic—it was a spiritual preparation."

"Next came the removal of the internal organs," he said, picking up a delicate bronze knife. "A small incision was made on the left side of the abdomen with a stone or obsidian blade. From there, the stomach, intestines, lungs, and liver were carefully extracted and placed into canopic jars." Working as he explained, he cut the "body" and extracted fake organs.

Several in the audience gagged. Others screeched. A few craven souls ran for the exit. Honestly, what did they expect?

"Each jar was guarded by a deity to ensure the organs' safety in the afterlife," Richard continued.

"The brain, however, was not so treasured," he said with a faint smile. "It was removed through the nostrils using this rather unpleasant tool—" he held up a hooked implement "—and was usually discarded."

More movement behind me told me some people had reached their limit.

I couldn't help but wrinkle my nose.

"Once emptied, the body was covered entirely in natron —a mixture of salts used to draw out all moisture. This drying process took forty days. It was, in effect, the ancient world's most effective desiccant."

"Then came anointing. The body was cleansed of natron and rubbed with oils and resins to keep the skin supple."

With the help of his assistant, he demonstrated the process. "It was during this stage that the priests would begin the ritual wrapping—layer upon layer of linen strips, often with protective amulets nestled within. Each amulet served a different purpose: safety in the afterlife, health, or even guidance."

He held up a small scarab charm with reverence. "And always, incantations from the *Book of the Dead* were recited throughout. These spells helped guide the soul safely through the Duat—the realm of the dead."

At last, he displayed a shimmering photograph of a golden death mask. "The final stage was to place a mask over the face of the deceased, preserving their identity for eternity. The wrapped body was then entombed within one or more coffins or sarcophagi, ready for its long journey to the afterlife."

When he concluded with another dramatic bow, the crowd rose in a thunderous standing ovation.

After acknowledging the accolades with a wave, Richard found us in the crowd.

Our beaming father slapped him on the back, while Mother warmly embraced him. "We're so proud of you, Richard."

"Impressive work," I said, kissing him on the cheek. "Though you might've warned me about the brain bit."

He chuckled. "And rob you of your reaction? Never."

After a quick introduction to Julian and brief words of congratulations from the family, he excused himself to change into formal clothes for the reception. Rather than wait for him, we proceeded to the private room where the previous one had been held. To no one's surprise, we found the air filled with excited conversations about Richard's presentation.

Julian Banks, catching sight of the gentleman he knew, excused himself after profusely thanking me for the introduction to Richard and the ticket to the lecture.

We didn't have long to wait for Richard to make an appearance. A few minutes after we arrived, he joined us. He should have been wearing a triumphant expression, given the success of his presentation. But he had turned somber.

"What's wrong?" I asked, wondering what had caused such a drastic change in him.

"Not here." He nodded to a spot which was relatively free of people, and we followed him. Behind the concealment of a large potted plant, he shared what was troubling him. "The meeting with the museum director and the curator of antiquities this afternoon did not go well."

"What happened?" I prompted.

"The vase Henderson brought to the meeting was not the same one I saw at the Great Hall. It was a clever substitution, one for which he had the right documentation. But that's not all."

My heart sank. I could well imagine what had happened. "You discovered more stolen pieces?"

He nodded. "I arrived early today and took a stroll through the Egyptian Hall. Several items on display should be in the Cairo Museum."

"Oh, Richard," Mother said. "How dreadful."

I came right to the point. "What are you going to do?"

"I have another meeting with the director tomorrow morning. I requested that Henderson not be present. I plan to walk him through the exhibition and point out the stolen objects."

Our family remained silent, absorbing the gravity of the situation. But finally, Father spoke, his voice steady and reassuring. "You're doing the right thing, Richard."

"Yes, as long as you're sure," I added, feeling a mix of pride and worry.

The peace of the moment, however, was short-lived. The curator had been mingling among the guests, soaking up accolades for achievements he hadn't earned. So deep in our conversation were we, none of us realized he'd not only approached, but had overheard our conversation.

"You're questioning my integrity?" Henderson screeched.

"I can only speak the truth," Richard answered.

"How dare you?"

His raised voice caught the attention of those nearby. As heads turned, the string quartet faltered, bows pausing mid-note. Conversations hushed as Martin Henderson—his face as red as the velvet drapery behind him—confronted Richard with fire in his eyes. "You've impugned my honor," he barked, jabbing a finger into Richard's chest.

Richard—never one to be intimidated—straightened to his full height, his mouth curling into a contemptuous sneer. "I've only stated what is true. The vase was stolen, its provenance fabricated."

As a collective gasp swept through the room, I edged closer to Richard and Henderson. I didn't want to miss a word of their conversation.

Robert leaned in and whispered, "You may wish to observe but not get involved."

He knew me too well.

"I showed you my documentation," Martin said. "Letters of authentication, shipping records, even a witness statement from the original owner's grandson. You may sling mud, Mister Worthington, but you'll find your hands dirtier than mine."

"You switched vases." Richard shot back, eyes gleaming with conviction. "The one you brought to the meeting was not the same one I saw at the Great Hall. That one was stolen. And that's not the only one. There are others."

"Say that again," Henderson spat out.

"I said," Richard's voice rose, echoing across the high ceiling, "you are a fraud, and your so-called acquisitions are stolen artifacts, likely smuggled out of Egypt under false pretenses."

A collective murmur rippled through the guests. Glasses clinked awkwardly, and the quartet wisely abandoned all pretense of music.

That's when the museum's director rushed over, arms half-raised like a man attempting to defuse a bomb.

"Gentlemen, please!" he hissed in a stage whisper that still somehow managed to carry across the room. "This is neither the time nor place—"

"He's slandering me in front of every patron in London," Henderson growled.

"And you're making a scene!" the director snapped, his calm façade fraying. "I will not have this reception devolve into a scandal fit for the broadsheets."

"He's the scandal," Richard muttered, pointing accusingly at Henderson.

"That's quite enough, Mister Worthington," the director said with forced patience. "I must ask you to leave."

As the air went still, Richard blinked, his face whitening with indignation. "You side with him?"

"I'm preserving the museum's dignity," the director replied tightly. "This display—this shouting match—is entirely unacceptable. You may voice your concerns in private tomorrow morning at ten in my office."

"We'll see how dignified the museum appears when the truth comes out," Richard said before turning to us. "Are you coming?"

"Yes, of course, dear," Mother answered for all of us.

As the throng made space for us, we marched out militant style. Silence lingered like a fog, heavy and awkward as we walked out of the reception. The music resumed, albeit hesitantly, and voices rose once more, carrying with them more than a hint of outrage and scandal. I couldn't help but feel there were bound to be repercussions from this night's event. And no one would come out the winner.

CHAPTER 8

A GRIZZLY DISCOVERY

*T*he Monday morning light streamed through the bay windows of our Eaton Square home, casting warm rays across the breakfast table where Robert and I were enjoying a start to our day. The aroma of freshly brewed coffee mingled with the scent of toasted bread, creating a serene atmosphere. I welcomed it, especially after the drama of the last few days.

On Saturday morning, Richard had met with the director who, after refusing to hear a word about the stolen artifacts, had given my brother his walking papers. Not content to terminate Richard's contract with the British Museum, he'd also forbidden him from even entering it again.

The argument at the reception had, of course, made the papers, especially the scandal rags who thrived on such things. One of the more illustrious journals was calling for an investigation into the British Museum's Egyptian acquisitions. Another was calling for the resignation of the museum director himself. But it hadn't stopped there. Ticket holders for Richard's lectures had rushed to the museum to demand refunds. Though they'd been assured that the lectures would continue, albeit with a different lecturer, they were not interested. It was Richard who'd been the draw, not some boring scholar.

As for me, I was ready, indeed eager, to attend to my detective agency duties. That, of course, included my investigation into Lady Miranda's disappearance.

"What are your plans for the day, darling?" Robert asked.

"I will be visiting the employment agency Lady Fallon used to hire Miss Fletcher, her daughter's companion. They should have her address. She would know better than anyone who Miranda talked to."

"She should be able to provide some of that information. But I doubt she'll know all of it."

I rested my cup on its saucer. "What do you mean?"

"From what you've shared, it strikes me that Miranda is quite an enterprising young lady. She managed to escape her home in the middle of the night. What's there to say she hadn't done that before? And if she did, she probably had help."

"Oh, I fully expect she did. This Isis woman was more than likely the contact. Miss Fletcher would have been present for that initial meeting. At the very least, she would be able to describe her."

Before he could comment, one of our footmen entered the dining room and addressed our butler. "Begging your pardon, Mister Black. The morning edition of *The Times* has arrived."

"Surely that can wait," our butler responded.

"There's an article on the front page that Lady Rutledge might want to see."

"Thank you, James," I said. "I'll take it."

The headline in bold, sensational print, screamed: "Mummified Remains Found in British Museum."

"Oh, dear." As I quickly scanned the article, my heart sank with every word. The victim was Martin Henderson, the very man Richard accused of stealing artifacts. The article hinted at dark deeds and cursed relics, the kind of story that sold papers, whether it was true or not.

"What is it, Catherine?" Robert asked, his voice filled with concern.

Before I could answer, the trill of the telephone pierced the calm of our breakfast nook. I didn't have to wonder who was calling this early in the morning. I knew. I rushed out of the dining room and picked up the receiver.

"Good morning, Mother."

"Have you read *The Times*?" she asked, her voice thick with panic.

As Robert joined me, he placed a comforting hand on my shoulder. "I have."

"They're going to arrest Richard!"

"Are the police there?" That would be dire indeed.

"No. But they will be."

The knot in my stomach eased somewhat. We had some time. "I'm coming over. We'll sort this out," I assured her, trying to keep my voice steady.

"Is Scotland Yard there?" Robert asked. He knew better than anyone what that meant.

"No. But I expect they'll soon make an appearance. Mother is panicking."

"Understandably so."

"I have to go."

"We'll both go. I'm not letting you go through this alone."

I embraced him. "Thank you." As a chief detective inspector, he would be able to provide us with invaluable advice.

In no time at all, we were making our way to

Worthington House, where Mother, Father, and Richard waited for us in the drawing room. While Mother's face was as pale as a ghost, Richard wore an expression of bewildered anger. Father stood beside him, his features set and stoic.

"Kitty, I didn't do this. I swear it," were Richard's first words as we entered.

"I know you didn't. Do you know how the body was discovered?"

He nodded. "Branson called me. You met him. He was helping me set up the various items in the Great Hall."

"I remember. What did he say?"

"Early this morning, a mummy was found in an open coffin in the Egyptian Hall. It was clear it was not part of the exhibit."

"Why?"

"It was, for lack of a better word, fresh. Genuine mummies are shriveled, their wrappings brown with age. This one was encased in pristine linen cloth. The exhibit was shut down, and the police were called. That's all he was able to tell me."

"Henderson was at the reception three days ago. Can a body be mummified that fast?"

"No. You were present at my lecture. It takes seventy days to prepare a mummy for the afterlife."

"Must have been done Saturday and Sunday then," Robert said matter-of-factly.

"Yes. It stands to reason," Richard agreed.

"Where were you during that time?" Robert asked, taking over the interrogation.

"After I was told my services were no longer required Saturday morning, I came home."

"Anyone who can vouch for that?"

"You won't take my word for it?" Richard asked some-what affronted.

"It's a question the police will ask, Richard," I said. "Best have a ready answer."

"Mother and Father. They were waiting for my return. Oh, and the footman who opened the door."

"Mildred and I can attest to that," Father said.

"What about afterwards?" Robert prodded.

"I headed out."

"Where did you go?"

Richard's face flushed. "I'd rather not say."

"What about Sunday?"

"Same."

The fool! "Richard, an arrest may be imminent," I said. "You must tell us where you went and what you did."

"I can't."

"It's a woman, isn't it?" I asked. "For heaven's sakes, Richard, you must tell us."

"It's *not* a woman," he gritted out through clenched teeth.

Before we could question him further, a sharp rap on the door interrupted us. Mister Carlton, Mother's butler.

"Begging your pardon, ma'am. Chief Inspector Withers wishes an audience with Mister Richard."

Robert turned to Richard, "Don't say more than is needed."

"Please show him in, Mister Carlton," Mother said with a resigned sigh.

Withers, seemingly into his late forties, going by his salt and pepper hair, cut a fine figure. Well-cut trousers, a matching vest, a jacket that hinted at Savile Row tailoring. A thoughtfully chosen tie and shoes polished to a mirror shine completed the image of a distinguished detective. He wasted no time taking in the people in the room. "I hope I'm not interrupting a family gathering. If I am, I apologize."

His affable manner was probably meant to put us at ease. No chance of that, especially Mother.

"Ah, Sinclair," Withers said with a twinkle to his eye. "Didn't expect to find you here."

"Withers," was all that Robert said. "What can we do for you?"

"Coming right to the point, I see. Very well. I'd like to speak to Richard Worthington. I understand he resides here."

Richard stepped forward. "I'm Richard Worthington."

"Splendid. Is there a private room where we can talk?"

"Whatever you have to say, you can do it in front of my family."

"As you wish."

"I'm Mrs. Worthington, Richard's mother. And this—" she pointed to Father "—is Mister Worthington, Richard's father. If you would please take a seat."

"Of course, ma'am." While Withers accommodated himself in a wingback chair, Robert and I made use of the settee. Mother sat on a sofa while Richard and Father remained standing.

After retrieving a notebook from his coat, Withers took a few moments to read over his notes. "This morning, I was called to the British Museum. Mummified remains were found in the Egyptian Exhibit. Turned out to be Martin Henderson, the curator of Egyptian Antiquities. Do you know anything about that, Mister Worthington?"

"No."

"When was the last time you saw Mister Henderson?"

"Doctor," I interceded. "Doctor Henderson."

"Thank you, er, Miss . . . "

"Lady Rutledge," Robert said. "My wife."

"Oh, yes, of course." He jotted something in his notebook.

"Friday night was the last time I saw him," Richard said.

"Yes, I understand you had a . . . falling out with him."

"You might say so."

Robert cleared his throat, a reminder that Richard shouldn't volunteer more information than was necessary.

"What was the nature of that conversation?"

"We disagreed about the provenance of several items in the museum."

"Please explain."

"I thought several pieces had in fact been stolen from the Cairo Museum. He disagreed."

"He took offense, did he?"

"Yes. He would, after all, have been the one who obtained them."

"The conversation was conducted in a public setting?" Withers asked.

"The reception after my lecture," Richard confirmed.

"What happened after your discussion?"

"The Director of the British Museum asked me to leave. At a meeting the following morning, he notified me that my services were no longer needed. I'd signed up for ten lectures. Had only presented two."

"The most recent one being on mummification."

Richard merely nodded.

"So, it could be said you're an expert on the subject?"

"You might say so. As an expert, I can tell you, no one can be mummified in so short a time. It takes roughly seventy days to mummify a body."

"Oh, it was clear he wasn't fully mummified," Withers said. "He'd been simply wrapped in linen. Together with the blood, it was enough to produce the desired shocking effect." Withers glanced down at his notes. "Where were you Saturday and Sunday, Mister Worthington?"

"After the meeting with the director, I came home. My parents were anxious to hear about the outcome. After that, I went for a walk."

"Where to?"

"Grosvenor Square."

"And then?"

"I can't tell you."

Father groaned. "For the love of God, Richard, tell him where you were."

"I can't because I don't know."

"What do you mean?" Robert asked.

"Sinclair, I'm conducting this enquiry," Withers reminded Robert.

"Yes, of course. My apologies."

"All I remember is walking toward Grosvenor Square, my thoughts a jumbled fog. Then—nothing. The next thing I knew, I was blinking awake on a cold, splintered bench, the sky above me black as ink. Midnight had long since fallen. My hands were numb, my stomach hollow with hunger. I stumbled through the streets like a ghost, drawn by instinct alone."

He had a gift for description, my brother.

"When I reached the house, I slipped around to the back —thank God I still remembered where the spare key was hidden beneath the loose stone. I crept into the larder, snatched whatever I could find with shaking fingers, and wolfed it down. I climbed the service stairs in the dark. By the time I reached my room, I could hardly walk. I didn't even remove my shoes—I simply collapsed onto the bed, still dressed, and let the blackness swallow me whole."

"Well, that's certainly an interesting tale," Withers said, a disbelieving tone to his voice.

"It's the truth!"

"Your family didn't report you missing?"

"It's happened before, Inspector," Mother rushed to say. "Several times, as a matter of fact. Richard spent the last several years in Egypt excavating archeological sites. He's used to being outdoors. So he goes on rambles. We did worry the first time it happened. Not so much afterwards. We knew he'd come home sooner or later."

"Very well," Withers said, coming to his feet. "That's all for now." He nodded to Mother. "Thank you for your hospitality, Mrs. Worthington." And then he turned to Richard. "Don't leave London. I will have more questions."

After he walked out the door, Mother clutched my arm, her eyes wide with fear. "Kitty, please, you must do something. Robert, you too. Richard's innocent!"

I squeezed her hand. "We will, Mother. Robert and I will find out what happened."

"First thing that needs to be done is to telephone Sir Frederick," I said. The barrister who'd represented Robert when he'd been accused of murder was not only one of the best barristers in the city but a client of my detective agency.

"Absolutely," Robert said.

"I'll take care of that now," Father said, rushing out. He was fully aware of Sir Frederick's telephone number. He'd been instrumental in obtaining the barrister's services for Robert.

I glanced up at Robert. "We'll need to visit the museum so we can examine the crime scene itself."

"We won't be allowed anywhere near it, at least for now. But we can talk to whoever found the body."

"Shall I go with you?" Richard asked, forgetting he'd been denied access.

"You can't go anywhere near the British Museum," Robert said. "The police will charge you with interfering. Stay home and try to remember where you were those two days."

"You shouldn't leave the house at all," I said. "The press will be camped outside the driveway waiting to pounce on you if you emerge."

"Surely, it won't be that bad," Richard said, an incredulous tone in his voice.

"No, it will be worse." As I had good cause to know.

Richard sighed heavily. "Very well. I will remain behind doors. By Jove, imprisoned in my own home."

"It won't be forever, Richard."

"Until when, then?"

"Until we find whoever murdered Henderson, of course." I prayed it wouldn't take us long. I doubted Richard would agree to be confined for more than a week.

CHAPTER 9

THE INVESTIGATION BEGINS

*A*fter a brief stop at home so I could fetch a fresh notebook and my satchel, Robert and I proceeded to the British Museum. The pavement buzzed with police activity and the morbidly curious. Nothing like a murder to bring out the crowds.

We would have been denied entrance except for Robert, who flashed his Scotland Yard credentials at the police officer guarding the door. As we stepped through the entrance, the grandeur of the neoclassical columns did little to ease the knot of unease growing in my stomach. Perhaps it was the knowledge that somewhere within, Henderson's remains had been discovered, transformed into a grotesque mimicry of an ancient Egyptian ritual. Or perhaps it was the knowledge that we were no longer merely visitors, but investigators.

"Do you suppose they'll let us into the Egyptian Hall?" I whispered to Robert.

"No. We'll need to find Richard's assistant. If anyone knows what happened, it'll be him. The docent might know where he can be found," he said nodding toward the information desk.

Catching sight of her, I turned around. "She knows I'm Richard's sister. Once she realizes that, she might very well deny us any information."

"Stay here then."

"Very well." Rather than stay rooted to that spot, as I was bound to attract notice, I strolled past the information desk seemingly with no particular destination in mind. But then that's what most museum visitors did. Once I'd moved past the desk, I turned to watch his interaction with the docent.

Wearing his most attractive smile, he approached the woman. After a brief conversation, she passed him a note.

Presumably, after having obtained the information we needed, he touched his fedora and winked at her before strolling toward me.

"Well?" I asked, once he reached my side.

"His office is close to the Egyptian wing." He flashed the note at me. "She drew me a map."

I noted a little heart on the upper corner. Honestly! I would need to talk to him once we returned home. His actions were bound to make him more memorable. But then he would be anyway. No living, breathing female could forget him when he turned on the charm.

We moved quietly past the Assyrian wing, stopping briefly to admire a carved relief. As we walked past the Egyptian Hall, we could see it'd been cordoned off. A thick velvet rope hung across the archway, and a sign read: *Closed for Investigation*. In case someone decided to intrude, two police officers stood at the entrance. A deterrent indeed.

Before our presence could alert suspicion, Robert led me through a side corridor. Moments later, we found Branson's office. After a quick knock, he opened the door. As soon as he recognized me, his expression grew wary.

"Mr. Branson," I said, "I hope you remember me."

"Of course I do. You're Mister Worthington's sister."

"That's right." I flashed him a friendly smile, hoping to put him at ease. "This is my husband, Robert Crawford Sinclair. He's a Chief Detective Inspector at Scotland Yard."

Robert extended a hand. "A pleasure to meet you, Mister Branson."

"Likewise," he said, taking it. "What can I do for you?"

"We're hoping to have a word about this morning's events. We understand this must be a difficult time."

Branson gave a dry laugh. "That's putting it mildly." He glanced around. "I'll be glad to talk with you, but best have this discussion in a spot where we won't be interrupted. If you would follow me."

"Of course," I answered, glad that he was willing to discuss what had transpired.

He led us down a narrow staircase to a basement hallway. The hum of old pipes echoed overhead, and the smell of dust and something more metallic—perhaps the scent of preserved artifacts—clung to the air. Finally, he pushed open a door to reveal a room stacked with floor-to-ceiling shelves filled with crates, statues, and other precious objects.

"As you can see—" Branson pointed to the shelves "—this is where we keep the items not on display. "Staff are the only ones who know it exists."

"Do you believe this is how they smuggled the body into the museum?" I asked.

Branson nodded grimly. "Best guess. The security guards —bless them—do a fine job upstairs. But they don't patrol down here. No one really does."

Robert knelt near a wooden crate. "Could someone access the Egyptian Hall from here?"

"Yes. There's a service stairwell down the corridor we just traveled that leads to a small door at the back of the hall. It's mostly used by curators and workmen when moving exhibits and is rarely locked. Whoever carried Henderson's remains into the hall more than likely would have used that door."

I swallowed hard, imagining the macabre scene: the body, hidden in some crate or bag, carried silently through the gloom, up into the hall that celebrated the afterlife, only to be staged as part of some horrifying tableau.

"Tell us about the discovery," I said softly. "What exactly happened?"

Branson leaned against a crate, clearly shaken. "I was supposed to meet with Doctor Henderson early this morning in the Egyptian Hall. He was planning on taking over Mister Worthington's lectures and wanted to choose the artifacts he would use. Only . . ." He paused, running a hand through his hair. "Only when I arrived, the Hall was locked. I had a key, of course, and I let myself in. I thought he was running late. But he wasn't. He was already there."

My breath caught. "Just not alive."

Branson nodded. "In a coffin. At first, I thought it was one of the mannequins we'd used for your brother's demonstration. But then I saw the blood. And the jars."

He turned pale just recalling it.

"They'd cut him open. Removed his organs. Placed them in canopic jars—real ones, ancient, from our own collection. They'd been positioned around the coffin, just like the ones we'd used for the lecture."

Robert's brow furrowed. "Who had access to the jars?"

"Only staff. Myself. Richard. And a few others with clearance. But I checked the records. The jars weren't signed out. They must've been taken after hours. Someone knew the layout well enough to take what they needed and cover their tracks."

I paced a few steps. "Whoever did this has to be familiar with the mummification process as well as have access to the hall." I glanced at Robert. "It has to be someone who works here at the museum."

"Or someone who knows someone who works at the museum."

Branson looked at me, his eyes haunted. "It was ritualistic. Intentional. Whoever did this wanted it to look exactly like an ancient mummification—gruesome as it was."

"Two questions come to mind," Robert said. "Who hated Henderson so much they ended his life in such a way, and who would have the knowledge to turn him into a mummy?"

"We don't have enough information to even start to guess," I said.

Branson gave a half-nod. "Henderson wasn't exactly beloved. Brilliant, yes. But he stepped on toes. Especially when it came to his theories."

"Which were?"

"He believed the Egyptians had help—outside help—in their development of embalming and afterlife rituals. He hinted at something more . . . esoteric."

Somewhat confounded, I tilted my head. "You mean like . . . aliens?"

Branson laughed. "No, not aliens. Ancient wisdom was passed down from older civilizations that belonged to other lands. He had a following—students who adored him—but also critics who said he was veering too far into mysticism."

I exchanged a look with Robert. "Sounds like someone might have wanted to discredit him in the most shocking way imaginable."

"That's the conclusion I keep coming back to," Branson said. "But how did they manage to move the body, set the stage, and leave without a trace?"

"That's what we intend to find out," Robert said. "We'll

need a list of all staff who have access to this storage area, especially in the past week."

"I can get that for you. There weren't that many. No new exhibits were added during that time."

"Was there any sign of forced entry?"

Branson shook his head. "None. Which means either someone had keys . . . or someone let them in."

The word hung in the air like a challenge: 'accomplice.' It had to be. Henderson was not exactly fat, but he had carried a bit of weight. No single man could have transported him. This was a two-man job. Or woman.

"Did Henderson have any enemies, or people who strongly disliked him?"

"Enough to kill in such a gruesome manner, you mean?"

"Yes."

"He was not liked, as I mentioned. But no one would commit a murder over a mere dislike." He paused for a moment. "Recently, though . . ."

"Yes," I prompted.

"Two days ago, I saw Dr. Henderson arguing with a man I didn't recognize. It got heated."

"What was the argument about?"

"I caught only a few words—*Not enough. I want more.* When they saw me watching, they glared at me before slipping into Henderson's office and slamming the door behind them."

"Ummm," I said. A falling out between thieves would be my guess. The swarthy gentleman may have been the one who obtained the stolen artifacts. Whatever Henderson had paid for them had not been enough.

I retrieved my notebook. "Could you describe him?"

"Olive skin, well-dressed, but in a foreign way, rings on every finger and a gold chain peeking out from under his shirt collar."

"Did you happen to catch a name?"

"Hassan el-Masri," Branson said. "He was wearing a badge with his name on it. Must have attended Henderson's *Sacred Symbols and Silent Stones* lecture held earlier that day."

"That should make it easier to locate him," I said. "Anything else you can think of, Mister Branson?"

He brushed a hand across his brow. "Not at the moment. No."

"If you do—" I retrieved my business card from my satchel "—please telephone me. If I'm not there, leave a message with the receptionist."

"I will." After a quick glance, he tucked the card into his jacket.

"Thank you for your assistance," I said.

"You're welcome. I hope you find Henderson's killer. He wasn't the most pleasant of men, but no one should die in such a gruesome way."

"We'll do our best," I said.

As Robert and I emerged into the museum's upper galleries, sunlight streamed through the high windows, catching the motes of dust in the air. For all its grandeur, the museum suddenly seemed like a tomb.

Only when we were in a taxicab did I speak. "It's like something out of a penny dreadful," I whispered. "A body cut open and left as a message."

Robert slipped his hand into mine. "It's also a clue. Whoever did this wanted people to see it. Now we just need to understand why."

This investigation was not just about a murder. It was about symbolism, obsession—and something far older and darker than either of us had imagined.

CHAPTER 10

A FAMILY BREACH

*B*y that evening, Robert had used his connections at Scotland Yard to obtain details about Hassan el-Masri. Turned out he was an Egyptian national who'd been in the UK for several years and known in certain circles for trading in rare antiquities—some authentic, others dubiously acquired. He ran a small office in a nondescript building off Euston Road, purportedly dealing in 'cultural curiosities.'

We made our way there the next morning.

The building was unnervingly still—so still it felt as though the walls themselves were holding their breath. Our footsteps echoed up the stairwell, each creak of the old wood louder than it had any right to be. Overhead, a lone bulb flickered with a sickly buzz, casting shadows that jittered like ghosts along the walls.

When we reached the landing, the door to Hassan's office

stood slightly ajar, tilted open just enough to suggest something was wrong—terribly wrong. My pulse quickened.
Robert moved ahead, silent but tense, and with a glance that
warned me to stay back, nudged the door open with the toe
of his shoe. His right hand hovered near his coat pocket. I
knew what was there—a revolver, small but deadly. Just in
case. God help us, I hoped we wouldn't need it.

What we found was a grim scene.

A man, whom we could only assume was Hassan, lay
sprawled across his desk, a dark pool staining the papers
beneath him. His face was twisted in shock, as though
surprised by death itself. I clutched Robert's arm to steady
myself. The air smelled of incense, blood, and something
fouler—preservative chemicals I would later learn.

My heart sank. I had hoped—foolishly, perhaps—that
Richard couldn't possibly be tied to another death. That
whatever madness he'd stumbled into had ended with
Henderson. But that hope was short-lived.

It was Robert who found the hidden door. Behind a
tapestry of Anubis guiding souls to the underworld was a
small back room. The stench of resin and embalming oils
was overwhelming. I covered my nose with my handkerchief
as we stepped inside.

On a worktable were linen wrappings, empty canopic
jars, and chalk markings matching the ones used in Richard's
demonstration. There were surgical tools and strange
powders, some labeled in Arabic. Most damning of all was a
bloodied robe, folded carefully beside a stack of journals—
and atop those, a wallet I recognized. Richard's.

Oh, dear God.

Jaw clenched, Robert stared at it for a long moment.
"Your brother was here."

"Against his will, more than likely unconscious," I rushed

to say, my heart beating wildly. My sweet, dear brother couldn't have killed Henderson in this horrid room. "Someone drugged him, brought him here. They performed that gruesome murder. And then took him back to Grosvenor Square once they delivered Henderson to the museum." I clutched Robert's arm. "It wasn't him."

Robert bracketed my shoulders with his strong hands. In a very kind voice, he spoke the words I knew would be coming, "We have to notify the police."

I glanced at the wallet. If it disappeared, the police would never know Richard had been here. Gazing back at him, I pleaded, "Couldn't we?"

"We can't tamper with the evidence, Catherine. You know that."

Yes, I did, but how I wished he wasn't such an honorable man.

The police and Inspector Withers, arrived within the hour. Between the physical evidence and Richard's wallet, it would be only a matter of time before my brother was taken into custody.

After an hour of questioning, the inspector released us. But not before forbidding us from contacting any member of my family, especially Richard, about what we'd discovered. As much as my heart ached to do so, I gave him our word. We returned home and waited for the ax to fall.

That afternoon, Mother telephoned with the news. As expected, Richard had been arrested.

"Inspector Withers told us you found another body—a Mister Hassan—and clear evidence that pointed toward your brother." The pain in her voice was unbearable. "You knew, didn't you, Kitty? You and Robert knew Richard would be arrested."

My breath hitched. "We didn't know, Mother." But we had suspected. The evidence was too damning.

"You didn't tell your father and me."

"We couldn't. Inspector Withers asked us not to."

"The law means more to you than your own family." Her tone was glacial.

"It doesn't." I took a breath, trying desperately to separate my emotions from logical thought. "Mother, please. I'd like to come and explain."

"There's nothing you can say that would excuse what you've done. Your father and I will be hiring an investigator to prove Richard's innocence. As much as it pains me to say this, for the time being, it would be best if you kept your distance."

"Mother!" But she didn't hear me. She'd ended the call.

"What did she say?" Robert's voice was tinged with concern.

"Richard's been arrested. She and Father are hiring an investigator. And she wants us to stay away." I dissolved into tears in Robert's arms.

"She'll come around, darling, you'll see."

"No, she won't. She thinks I betrayed her. In her eyes, that's the worst thing I could have done."

"You did not betray her or Richard. You allowed Inspector Withers to follow the evidence where it led. If we'd hidden that wallet and he found out, we would have been tossed in gaol ourselves. And then we wouldn't be able to investigate this murder."

My breath hitched as I glanced up at him. "*We're* going to investigate?"

"Of course, we are." That smile that made me melt made an appearance. "After all, I have nothing better to do."

I let out a watery laugh. "Oh, yes, you have so much free time. Never mind all the responsibilities you inherited."

He tenderly brushed a curl away from my cheek. "It can all wait. This is more important. You are more important."

The telephone rang once more, the private line in my parlor. Could it be Mother again? Collecting myself, I picked up the receiver. "Hello."

"Miss Worthington?" Lady Fallon. I recognized the voice. Probably wanted to know what progress I'd made.

"Yes. Good afternoon."

"I'm afraid it's not, at least for you. I just learned your brother has been arrested for that gruesome murder at the British Museum."

How on earth had she heard that so quickly? Did she have a connection at Scotland Yard? Regardless, I had to defend my brother. "It's a mistake. He's quite innocent."

"Maybe so. But the press will sensationalize it. The scandal will be all everyone will talk about. One I don't wish to touch the Fallon name and Miranda. So, I'm terminating your services. Please send me an invoice for the work you've done. I'll make sure it's immediately paid. Thank you, Miss Worthington. Goodbye."

"Goodbye."

Robert stood next to me, his brow raised in question.

"Lady Fallon has dismissed me. She doesn't wish her family to be connected to the notoriety Richard's arrest will bring."

"She's done you a favor. You can now dedicate all your time to investigating the murders without another matter to worry about."

I smiled at him. "Well, that's one way of looking at it."

"The only way." He took my hand, curled it around his elbow. "Now, I don't know about you, but I'm feeling a bit peckish. How about we ask our wonderful staff to serve our tea here? While we're eating, we can plan our next steps."

"That sounds wonderful." It'd been hours since breakfast.

But before we could put action to words, Mister Black made a sudden appearance. "You have a visitor, milady."

I didn't have to wait long to find out who it was. "Ned!"

My oldest brother barely paused long enough to say, "Kitty, Robert," before he continued with "What are we going to do about Richard?"

"Funny you should ask. We were just about to hold a strategy session."

"Count me in."

"Mother telephoned. She's rather upset with me." I glanced at Robert. "With us."

"She's afraid of what could happen to Richard," Ned said in a kind voice. "Understandably so. Father and Lily are providing what comfort they can. The best thing we can do for her and Richard is get on with the investigation. Once we start showing progress, she'll come around."

"I hope so," I said, not entirely sure she would.

"Let's move this discussion to the library," Robert suggested. "Oh, and Mister Black, could you please have our tea served there?"

"Certainly, milord."

No sooner had we settled in that room than Mister Black appeared once more. Before he could even say a word, I asked, "Another visitor?"

"Indeed, milady."

Lady Mellie this time. Hollingsworth's sister. Of course, she couldn't stay away. "I hope you don't mind. I came as soon as I heard."

"What about your assignment?" Now a trainee assistant lady detective, she'd been researching newspaper archives.

"All done. I passed the information to Lady Aurelia. She'll take it from there. There's nothing pressing now," Mellie rushed to say. "If something urgent comes up, she'll telephone."

"Very well. If you're sure." As busy as we were, I hated to take staff from the work of the agency.

"Oh, and Emma is on her way back from Oxfordshire. Apparently, she found the information she needed. She'll be here tomorrow."

"With Marlowe in tow, I would imagine."

Mellie grinned. "Can you doubt it?"

CHAPTER 11

THE INVESTIGATIVE COMMITTEE MEETS

"So, what do we know?" Ned asked once we'd settled into the library and enjoyed our tea.

Robert and I took turns describing the events as we knew them, ending with the discovery of Hassan's body.

"The wallet was definitely Richard's?" Ned asked.

"Absolutely. It's the brown leather one he bought at a Cairo bazaar. Full grain leather, the color of aged chestnut. A lotus flower imprinted on the corner. There's no doubt it was his."

"Still, it could belong to someone else."

"His initials were carved into the leather, Ned."

He blew out a breath. "Well, that nails it."

"Yes, it does. The question becomes how it arrived there."

"Well, obviously, he was kidnapped, given some . . . drug that erased his memory."

I could very well believe it. During a previous investigation, a witness had gone missing. When we found her, she had no recollection of where she'd been. The hollow look in her eyes had haunted me for weeks.

"Barbiturates were used to interrogate our agents during the war," Ned continued. "Not only do those drugs cause memory loss, but they can inflict substantial damage."

"Oh, dear God. Richard. Could he be permanently affected?" My stomach clenched at the thought. He was my brother. Arrogant, maddening, and stubborn—but he didn't deserve this. No one did.

"Once I found out about his memory loss, I insisted he be examined by Doctor Crawley. Mother and Father had no idea that had happened. They believed he was with a woman and didn't want to own up to it in front of Mother." He turned to Mellie. "Sorry. I shouldn't have said that."

Somewhat affronted, Mellie said, "I know what men and women do, Ned. No need to wrap things in clean linen for me."

"Henderson's mummy linens most certainly were not clean," I said in an attempt to lighten the mood.

When my humor landed, everyone laughed. And just like that, the tension was broken.

"Yes, well, err." Ned cleared his throat. "In any case, Doctor Crawley did not see any sign of permanent impairment. But he advised us to keep an eye on him."

"Something that will be hard to do now that he's in jail. No wonder Mother was so upset."

"Exactly. So, what's the strategy?" he asked.

"Our theory is that Hassan sold stolen antiquities to Henderson. They had a difference of opinion as to the price, and Henderson ended up dead."

"Does Hassan have the required knowledge to mummify a body?"

"No idea. That's something we'll need to find out." I wrote

that item in the investigation notebook I'd already begun. "We should start with Hassan's known associates."

"I can find that out from Scotland Yard," Robert said. "They have a file on him."

"You won't get in trouble?" I asked.

"Don't worry. I'll call in favors."

"Very well. What about Henderson?" I asked. "Who hated him so much that they murdered him in such a gruesome way?"

"It does look rather personal," Ned said.

"A woman?" Mellie suggested. "Or someone he betrayed?"

A chill crept over me. "Perhaps someone whose life he destroyed." I tapped my pen against the edge of the notebook. "Or a rival collector, perhaps, who was tired of losing to him."

"Good questions, with no answers. Yet," Robert said. "We need to find out more about him. Friends, enemies, lovers."

"I agree. Where do we start?"

"Henderson didn't get to be the curator of Egyptian Antiquities without someone recommending him. The British Museum Director will know," Ned suggested.

I shook my head. "Richard tarnished the reputation of the museum. And now he's been arrested for Henderson's murder. He won't talk to us."

"What about Julian Banks?" Robert asked.

"Who's that?" Mellie asked.

"A young man I met in connection with another matter. He studied archaeology at Oxford and was seeking an introduction to Richard."

"He may have admired Henderson," Ned said.

I shook my head. "He never said such a thing. He has contacts at Oxford, and his professor gave him the names of scholars living in London. He may be able to help. It's thin, but it's a lead."

"What about antiquities dealers?" Mellie asked. "There must be a few of those in the city. They would have had cause to deal with Hassan."

"Great suggestion, Mellie," I said.

"Worthington & Son has several clients who purchase rare objects. For valuation purposes, they submit not only what they own but the price they paid and where they obtained it."

"Wouldn't that be a violation of client confidentiality?" Robert asked.

"I wouldn't share the clients' names, only the names of the establishments."

"That should be fine, Robert," I said.

A raised eyebrow, but he nodded. "Very well."

Silence fell over the room for a beat. Each of us lost in our own thoughts, as the shadows of doubt crept in.

"I can't stop thinking about the mummification," Mellie said softly. "That wasn't just murder. It was . . . ceremonial. Like a message."

"A warning, perhaps?" I asked.

"Or a reenactment," Robert added grimly. "What better way to hide a crime than behind the veil of history?"

The words chilled me to the core. But I put my feelings aside. We had to move forward. "So how do we divide the investigation?"

"I'll contact Scotland Yard about Hassan," Robert said. "Ned will search through his clients' records to find antiquities shops. You and Mellie visit Julian Banks and see what you can find out about this Isis cult."

"Excellent plan, darling," I said, beaming at him. It was good to see him occupied in something that challenged his intellect.

As the late afternoon sunlight faded into dusky blue, we decided to adjourn. Our little task force was weary but determined. We would meet again tomorrow at four. Hopefully, that would give us sufficient time to discover some piece of truth in this tangled knot of murder, memory, and myth.

For if we didn't find answers soon—someone else might end up dead.

CHAPTER 12

REVELATIONS

$\mathcal{U}$pon our arrival at Julian Banks' home shortly before eleven the next morning, I exchanged a quick glance with Lady Mellie. "Ready?" I asked.

"Of course. I'm looking forward to meeting the gentleman and hearing what he has to say."

Our brief knock drew an immediate response. Same as before, Julian opened the door himself. Unlike last time, when he'd been dressed like a proper gentleman, his sleeves were now rolled up and his hair mussed as if he'd been running his hands through it for hours. I recognized the signs. The gentleman had become engrossed with something.

"Miss Worthington, welcome to my home once more. Please come in," he said, opening wide the door.

In the foyer, I said, "May I introduce Lady Mellie. She's helping with our enquiries."

After a brief pause, he inclined his head. "A pleasure, Lady Mellie." Going by his dumbfounded expression, he seemed quite struck by her. Not that it was a surprise. Her stunning red-haired, blue-eyed beauty tended to captivate most gentlemen.

Rather than lead us to the drawing room I'd visited before, he took us to a large chamber filled with ancient texts and dusty papers. A stack of archaeological journals sat willy-nilly on top of a massive desk with an open notebook filled with handwriting scrawls next to it. Had to be his study.

Mellie wrinkled her nose at the faint smell of ink and old paper, but I was rather delighted. It felt like we were about to unearth something important.

"Excuse the dirt," Julian said. "I was doing some research."

"And did you find anything?" I asked hopefully.

"Indeed, I did. But where are my manners? Please take a seat." He pointed to two brown leather chairs which had been rather haphazardly cleaned. One bore the imprint of a book, while the other clearly showed paw prints. A cat, going by their size and shape.

Mellie employed her handkerchief to clean the one with the book imprint. Unfortunately, Julian noticed.

"I apologize, Lady Mellie. I should have had it cleaned. But I became so immersed in my research, I lost track of the time."

She glanced at him with the sweetest smile. "No harm done, Mister Banks."

Of course, he gazed moony-eyed at her.

Best get right to the point. Sitting on the paw prints chair without preamble, I said, "What have you discovered, Julian?"

"Well, first, I must apologize. I should have called you right away when I heard what I did. But I wanted to do some research first. And then you telephoned, and well, it was the perfect opportunity."

He was making no sense. "If you could start at the beginning, Julian?"

"Yes, of course." He cleared his throat. "After your family departed the reception on Friday night, I remained behind to talk to my Oxford friend. The one who waved to me?"

"Indeed, I remember."

"While I was talking to him, I overheard a conversation. Two men and one woman. At first, I didn't think much of it. Everyone was discussing some topic about Egypt. But then one of the men called the woman Isis."

That got my attention! "He wasn't just talking about Osiris's wife?"

"No," he said, followed by, "Where is my notebook? I wrote it down as soon as I left. Ah, here it is."

He found it under the stack of journals.

"One of the men said, *The plans for the ceremony must be finalized, Isis.*"

"What ceremony?" Mellie asked.

"I wondered that too, so I remained rooted to the spot. Thankfully, my friend kept prattling on, so they didn't notice I was listening to their conversation. Of course, with the number of people in the room, I didn't hear every word. But I caught enough. To answer your question, it's a ceremony to awaken the god Osiris."

"Who's Osiris?" Mellie asked, a wrinkle to her brow.

"The Egyptian god of resurrection, among other things," Julian explained.

"Resurrection? They don't really believe that, do they?" Mellie asked somewhat dumbfounded.

"They apparently do. May I explain?"

"Of course," Mellie answered.

"Osiris was killed, dismembered, and brought back to life by his wife Isis. Going by the snippets of conversation I overheard, their cult believes that his resurrection is not only possible, but imminent. They appear to believe they're the ones who will bring it about. Not metaphorically—literally. Using ancient rites, blood sacrifice, the works."

A chill settled between my shoulder blades.

"Apparently, they have a willing subject," he went on. "Someone they called *"The Vessel"*. The ceremony is supposed to take place soon."

"Oh, good heaven," I said.

"One of the men mentioned Imhotep, the name of an Egyptian priest."

"What did he say exactly?"

"Imhotep has clearly become a problem. He must be dealt with."

"Dealt with?"

"'The sooner the better,' the other man said. The woman nodded in agreement.

"Could Imhotep have been Henderson?" I asked.

"Could very well be. He would have had the knowledge to perform such a ceremony."

"But what trouble could he have been causing?" I asked.

"No idea. He could have been trying to stop the ceremony or objected to the *Vessel*." He pointed to the stack of books. "The *vessel* has to be a young woman, a virgin." His face flushed as he glanced at Mellie. "Forgive me for mentioning such a thing in your presence."

"No need to ask for forgiveness, Mister Banks. My world view is not so narrow that I would be offended by the word. What I am, though, is horrified that a young woman would be murdered to supposedly bring about a god's resurrection. That is what they're trying to do?"

"Indeed," Julian said. "And I share your outrage."

While they'd been flirting with each other, I'd pondered the ramifications. "Richard was framed for Henderson's murder to prevent the investigation into the stolen artifacts from leading them to this cult."

"That's my thinking as well."

"A great theory," Mellie said, "but how do we go about proving it?'

"We'll need to find these people."

"That's where Professor Larchmont comes in," Julian said.

CHAPTER 13

VISIT WITH A SCATTERBRAINED SCHOLAR

*P*rofessor Larchmont's chambers occupied the entire fourth floor of a once-grand Bloomsbury townhouse, the kind with ornate cornices and iron-railed balconies that whispered of Victorian opulence. These days, however, the professor's domain bore the unmistakable mark of scholarly entropy—less curated gentleman's residence, more the lair of a brilliant, absent-minded collector who had long since abandoned order for obsession.

The narrow staircase that led to his quarters creaked with every step, and by the time we reached the top, the scent of ink, sandalwood, and something faintly toasted lingered in the air. Julian knocked twice. After a flurry of scuffling and a half-muffled curse, the door swung open.

"Mind the books," the professor warned immediately, as though we might stumble headfirst into a trap. And in truth, the danger was real enough.

The chamber beyond was a veritable jungle of scholarship. Piles of cracked-leather journals and hand-annotated texts teetered dangerously from every flat surface, including several chairs and an overturned hat stand now employed as a makeshift scroll rack. Bookshelves groaned under the weight of rare volumes—many of them unlabeled, others stacked sideways, backwards, or open to marked passages with entire conversations scrawled in the margins.

Interspersed among the academic clutter were the relics of ancient Egypt itself: a falcon-shaped statue missing half a wing, a tarnished ankh resting atop an untouched tray of toast, a gold-inlaid canopic jar serving as an impromptu paperweight. On one windowsill sat a sandstone bust of what I assumed to be an Egyptian goddess, gazing serenely down on the remains of breakfast—soft-boiled eggs now hardened in their cups, a forgotten pot of tea, and a precarious tower of marmalade-smeared plates.

And prowling among it all with the quiet arrogance of a feline pharaoh was a sleek black cat. He brushed against ancient papyri with all the heedless indifference of one who'd been worshipped in another life. At present, he was attempting to wedge himself behind a stack of hieroglyphic scrolls, tail flicking with deliberate menace.

"Anubis!" the professor barked, spotting the cat mid-destruction. "No crawling behind the Book of the Dead! We've had this conversation!"

The cat ignored him entirely and vanished into the shadowed clutter.

Mellie, understandably, looked both horrified and fascinated.

"Do forgive the mess," the professor said, sweeping his arms wide as if he'd just realized we were standing in what appeared to be the aftermath of an academic avalanche. "I find order to be terribly stifling to original thought."

I wasn't sure about that, but there was no denying the

place pulsed with curiosity. A kind of holy chaos. Every object had a story. Every paper, a secret. It felt like we'd stepped into the heart of some ancient mystery itself, buried not beneath desert sand, but beneath toast crumbs and ink blotches.

And in the center of it all, Professor Larchmont—brilliant, dithering, utterly absorbed—stood like a high priest of forgotten knowledge, ready to impart truths wrapped in riddles, footnotes, and tea-stained revelations.

"Julian Banks!" the professor cried, pushing his glasses up with an inky thumb and offering a beaming smile. "Haven't seen you since the New Kingdom lecture! Or was it the Third Intermediate Period?"

"I believe it was both, sir," Julian said, ushering Mellie and me into the room. "May I present Catherine Worthington and Lady Mellie?"

"Charmed, charmed, charmed," the professor said, giving three quick, jittery bows and knocking over a stack of papyrus in the process. "Do make yourselves at home. Oh— no, don't sit on that chair, my dear," he said to Mellie. "It's supporting the Hathor stele. Yes, that other one will do."

Mellie looked fascinated, if mildly alarmed. He beamed approvingly when she settled herself into a Georgian period armchair.

I perched on the edge of a worn, dusty leather seat, avoiding the delicate statuette resting beside it.

Julian got straight to the point. "Professor, I know you've been compiling research on fringe cults related to Egyptian mythology. We believe one such group may be active in London."

The professor's eyes lit up. "Isis. It's always Isis."

"Then you have heard of them?" I asked.

"Heard of them?" Larchmont exclaimed. "I've been tracing their movements since 1919. They're terribly secretive. Hard to pin down. But yes, I know who they are. Or at least—I know *some* of them."

My heart sped up. "Please, tell us everything."

"Well!" He clapped his hands and paced the room with great agitation. "To start, the Cult of Osiris is a modern interpretation—albeit a wildly distorted one—of the ancient Egyptian mysteries. They center their practices around the resurrection of Osiris and the sacred role of Isis in restoring life through ritual sacrifice."

"Sacrifice," Mellie repeated, her voice clipped. "You mean murder."

"Quite possibly," Larchmont said, unfazed. "The original myths are metaphorical, of course—death and rebirth, the cycle of the Nile, agricultural renewal. But this group . . . no, they take it literally. Blood, ritual, willing vessels—oh yes. I've intercepted letters. Cryptic messages. Mentions of 'The Awakening.' All very theatrical."

"Do you know who's involved?" I asked, leaning forward.

"Some. Not all." He scratched his chin. "One must always proceed cautiously when making allegations. But I do have . . . strong suspicions."

"Professor," Julian said gently, "two men are dead. Another wrongly accused. And a young woman's life may be in danger. We don't have the luxury of caution."

The professor grew suddenly still. His eyes, which had been jittery and blinking behind thick lenses, focused for the first time. "Then listen carefully."

We did.

"There is a core group," he said, moving to his cluttered desk and rifling through a series of notecards. "I believe it consists of five or six individuals. All prominent in one way or another—academics, collectors, and patrons of the arts. Their wealth and status shield them from scrutiny."

"Names," I pressed.

"Yes, yes. Here." He produced a dog-eared card. "Lord Ambrose Greyston. Wealthy antiquities collector. Has funded multiple digs in the Valley of the Kings. Eccentric, deeply spiritual. Suspected of smuggling artifacts."

"I know the name," Julian said grimly.

"Next—Dr. Thaddeus Berwick. Formerly of the British Museum. Brilliant Egyptologist but dismissed under rather hush-hush circumstances. Rumored to have dabbled in occult interpretations of hieroglyphics."

"Charming," Mellie muttered.

"And finally—Madame Celestine LeClair," Larchmont said, his voice dropping as if the name itself carried weight. "French medium. Claims to commune with the spirits. She hosts a salon in Mayfair. Has a devoted following—wealthy, influential, and utterly enthralled."

A chill rippled down my spine. "Isis?" I asked.

He hesitated, then gave a noncommittal shrug. "Possibly. I suspect 'Isis' is a title passed from one initiate to the next. But LeClair . . . she fits. Charismatic. Dangerous. She radiates conviction—truly believes she's a divine conduit. That kind of certainty is either delusion . . . or something far more troubling."

"You wouldn't happen to have her telephone number?" I asked, trying to sound casual, though my voice had gone thin. Greyston and Berwick were public figures—we could find them. But LeClair? It would take time, and that was something we did not have.

"Ah, yes. You'll need that," he murmured, rifling through the chaos of papers and half-written notes on his desk. The silence stretched. Then—"Aha!" He plucked a slip of paper free, holding it like a conjurer revealing a trick. "Here it is."

I took it from him with trembling fingers. "You really believe they're planning a resurrection ritual?" I asked quietly, already fearing the answer.

Larchmont met my gaze, and for once, the scatterbrained professor was deadly serious. "I don't just believe it. I'm certain of it. The vessel would be a woman—young, untouched. To be 'killed' as Osiris was and brought back to life through the combined energies of the cult."

"Superstitious nonsense," Julian muttered.

"Yes, but dangerous nonsense," Larchmont replied. "The line between ritual and reality blurs in their minds. They believe they are enacting sacred destiny. That makes them unpredictable."

"And potentially lethal," I added.

"Precisely."

Mellie leaned forward. "How soon would this ceremony take place?"

"I fear very soon," the professor admitted. "There are alignments—they follow lunar cycles. The next full moon is in four days. If they intend to carry out the ritual, it would be then."

Julian and I exchanged a glance. "Then we've no time to lose."

"Professor," I said, rising, "you've been invaluable. Thank you."

"Oh, you're quite welcome! Take anything you need—oh, but not Anubis. He bites."

We left him muttering to a canopic jar about misplaced translations, but we had what we needed.

Names. Dates. A lead on the woman called Isis.

And God willing, just enough time to stop a murder masquerading as mythology.

CHAPTER 14

SECOND MEETING OF THE INVESTIGATIVE COMMITTEE

fter bidding goodbye to Professor Larchmont, Mellie and I emerged from the house, my stomach gave a polite protest. No wonder. We'd completely missed our luncheon. But truthfully, I'd been too distracted by the professor's revelations to feel properly hungry. The cult, the resurrection rite, the notion of a willing sacrifice—it all sat like a stone in my chest.

Still, I knew we needed a moment to regroup, to eat something, and to think. So after bidding goodbye to Julian and offering our deep thanks for his assistance, Mellie and I returned to Eaton Square, where the familiar surroundings of home helped ease the tightness in my chest—if only slightly.

"Professor Larchmont was fascinating, but I could've eaten one of his dusty scrolls by the end," Mellie said as she collapsed onto the settee in my personal parlor.

"Should we order sandwiches?" I asked.

"Yes, please, and something sweet."

After taking care of that task, I paced near the fireplace, still too restless to sit. "If what Larchmont said is true, we might have only days."

"You're right," she agreed. "And that means we need Madame LeClair to agree to a séance tonight. She won't just fit us in because we sound desperate—though we are."

"She's more than likely theatrical. All mediums are. We'll need something irresistible." I chewed my lip. "Something tragic, mysterious . . . dripping in unresolved family drama."

"Well, you have plenty of that to spare." Mellie raised a brow. "What about your Aunt Vivienne?"

I stopped pacing and stared at her. "I don't have an Aunt Vivienne."

"Sure, you do," Mellie said with a grin.

I finally understood what she was trying to convey. "Sorry. Hunger pains are clouding my brain." I took a moment to dream up this fictional aunt. "She was like a second mother to me," I admitted, slowly. "Sharp as a whip, utterly glamorous, and never without a cocktail in one hand and a scandal in the other. She used to say I had a nose for secrets—even the ones no one wanted found."

"I like her already."

"She swore she'd taken care of everything before she died. Her will, her affairs . . . she said I wouldn't have to lift a finger."

"But?" Mellie prompted.

"But the will vanished. Not misplaced—gone. There's been no trace, no explanation. And without it, everything she meant to leave me is locked in limbo."

Mellie's eyes sparkled. "That's it, then. That's the story. A loving, eccentric aunt with a mysterious missing will. You need closure. You need guidance. And only Madame LeClair can help you speak to her beyond the veil."

"I wouldn't put it past dear Aunt Viv to haunt the solicitor who annoyed her."

Mellie smirked. "Now you're getting into the swing of things. Oh, I have an idea. Tell Madame LeClair that Aunt Vivienne has been seen. Glimpsed in mirrors. Her perfume lingers in locked rooms. She's trying to say something—something urgent."

"You're positively wicked," I said, reaching for the telephone. "But I adore you for it."

"I know. Now be sincere but distraught. Touch of a tremble in the voice. And don't forget to sound just unhinged enough to be interesting."

I dialed the number Professor Larchmont had provided with a sense of mischief and something else—trepidation. I needed this to work.

Madame LeClair's assistant answered on the third ring, her voice smooth and cool, like silk drawn over marble.

I didn't wait for pleasantries. The moment she gave her name, I launched into my story—my voice barely steady, trembling with just the right balance of desperation and decorum. I spoke of my beloved Aunt Vivienne, her sudden passing, the missing will, and the strange whispers in the night. And how, above all, I needed to speak with her tonight.

A weighted silence followed.

"I'm afraid that will be impossible," the assistant said at last, her tone clipped, professional. "Madame LeClair is already committed to a session this evening."

My breath caught. No. That couldn't be. Not when time felt so perilously short.

"I understand," I said, my voice tightening, "but this is urgent. There are matters left unresolved. A fortune hangs in the balance. I fear . . . I fear my aunt is trying to reach me."

The pause on the other end was longer this time. Almost wary.

"Very well," she said finally. "I will speak to Madame LeClair. If there is any shift in her schedule, you shall be informed."

Then the line went dead.

I had no time to wonder about that conversation as just then a footman arrived with a tray of sandwiches and pastries. A maid brought up the rear with the tea and coffee service.

While we satisfied our hunger, Mellie and I put together our heads to build on the story we'd devised and plan our disguises.

"I refuse to wear anything that smells like mothballs," Mellie declared, biting into a jam tart.

I stifled a laugh. "You'll look more convincing as a grieving spiritualist if you embrace the theatrical. Besides, the smell would add authenticity."

She arched a brow. "Authenticity is overrated. I'd rather not suffocate on vintage camphor fumes while trying to summon the dead."

Once we ended our meal, we proceeded to my dressing room to choose my outfit for the seance. There was quite a wide array to choose from—veils, lace gloves, and high-collared gowns in varying degrees of somber elegance. I raided the back of my wardrobe for the darkest pieces I owned—some worn only for funerals or terribly serious garden parties and chose the dowdiest one. As I gazed at myself in the mirror, I was horrified by what I saw. Stylish, it was not. Once the charade was done, I would donate it to charity.

Mellie, who was far curvier than I, would wear a dress Robert's valet had located from his treasure trove of theatrical clothing. Before coming to work for Robert, he'd worked as a costumer for a theatre company. Somehow, he'd managed to hang on to quite an extensive wardrobe.

"So who am I supposed to be?" she asked staring somewhat dubiously at the very serviceable gown.

"My companion?" I suggested.

"I'm younger than you!"

"My cousin, then. You're the reason I want to find Aunt Viv's will. You fell in love with a gentleman from the city. But he won't marry you without a dowry. With your family being as poor as the proverbial church mouse, well, you see the problem."

"Who's the beau?"

"Ned, of course."

Mellie's gaze widened. "Lily will skin me alive. He's her fiancé." Never mind that Mellie was Lily's best friend.

"No, she won't because she'll never find out. It's only for one night, Mellie."

She stepped behind the screen to change while I adjusted my own appearance in the mirror. A wig of dark chestnut curls sat atop the stand, and I eyed it critically. "I think I'll wear this."

Mellie peeked out. "The widow's wig? Excellent choice. It gives you an air of tragic romance. Like someone who's lost her husband in a terrible dirigible accident."

"Exactly the look I was going for," I said dryly.

"How do I look?" Mellie asked as she stepped out in her ensemble—a black gown with a touch of lace at the throat and sleeves, paired with a delicate veil that shadowed her aquamarine eyes just enough to be intriguing.

"Gorgeous, as always." She would be beautiful even wearing sackcloth and ashes.

She wrinkled her nose. "I'd rather be thought of as intelligent."

"Lucky for you, you are both."

"What name should I use?"

I stood back to gaze at her. "Well, I've already given my name as Catherine Marsh. You can be Melissa Marsh. Mellie for short." That would avoid any confusion in case either Ned or I slipped up.

"Throw in a family curse, and we'll have the full Gothic experience," she murmured, adjusting the veil over her face.

"Darling, we're attending a séance. Drama is the point." I was joking, of course—but under the layers of lace and clever banter, I felt something far heavier pressing against my chest.

Mellie must have sensed the shift because her tone softened. "Are you all right, Kitty?"

Meeting her gaze in the mirror, I summoned a smile. "Right as rain." The clock in my dressing room suddenly chimed the four o'clock hour. "Heavens, look at the time." The investigative committee meeting was scheduled for now.

As I made a dash for the door, Mellie stopped me. "You can't go dressed like that. You have to change. We both do."

"Right."

After putting ourselves to rights, we made our way down the staircase to find Ned perched by the fire with his notebook open and a pen poised like a rapier. A cup of coffee on the table next to him. His expression was all business—intelligent eyes scanning his scribbles with that signature furrow between his brows.

"Where's Robert?"

"He's running late," Ned said. "Mister Black took the message."

"Ah," I said, gazing out the window. "Maybe the weather has delayed him." The rain had begun again, falling in fine sheets against the tall windows of the library.

As it turned out, we did not have to wait long. Only a few minutes later, Robert stepped into the library, looking damp and cross with the London weather. "Sorry, darling. It's beastly out there." He gave me a subtle smile, the sort that warmed something deep in my chest, before crossing the room to kiss my cheek.

Even as he joined me on the sofa, the sounds of other guests filtered in from the foyer—voices raised, a few cross words muffled beneath the polite tones of arrival. Lady Emma and Lord Marlowe were shaking off their umbrellas like a pair of disgruntled spaniels and stamping wet boots on the entry rug.

"Sorry we're late," Emma announced as she and Marlowe swept into the room like a minor tempest. Her cheeks were flushed from the cold, but her energy—as ever—could have powered a small village.

"No need to apologize," I said, rising to greet them. "We're so glad you made it through the monsoon."

Robert gestured to the round table at the side of the room. "Please help yourselves to coffee or tea. It should help thaw you out."

Marlowe eyed the teapot with mild suspicion, as if it might bite. "Any chance we could upgrade to something distilled and slightly more persuasive?"

"Of course," Robert said, already on his feet. He poured a couple of fingers of brandy into a snifter and handed it over with the solemnity of a clergyman performing a sacrament.

Marlowe accepted it just as reverently. "Ah, now that's more like it. Tea warms the body—brandy revives the soul."

"And possibly singes the eyebrows," Emma added, wrinkling her nose as she helped herself to a far more sensible cup of Earl Grey.

The storm continued its quiet percussion beyond the glass panes while we arranged ourselves around the room. As neither Emma nor Marlowe had been in London for any of the events preceding the investigation, we took turns explaining what had transpired.

"So Richard was arrested for Henderson's murder, and more than likely Hassan's as well?" Emma asked.

"Yes."

"My, he has been busy. I'm jesting, of course."

"How was Oxfordshire?" I asked.

"The vicar is not the proper man of the cloth he's supposed to be. Licentious does not begin to describe him."

"And you have proof?"

Emma nodded. "Signed by witnesses, sealed by a notary, and delivered to Lady Hutton, who was extremely appreciative."

"Good." One less thing to worry about. "Mellie and I spoke to Julian Banks earlier today, and then we visited Professor Larchmont. Julian arranged the meeting. The professor is . . . eccentric, but extremely knowledgeable. He confirmed that the Cult of Osiris exists. He mentioned a resurrection ritual—rare, dramatic, and usually symbolic—but in this case . . ."

"In this case," Mellie finished for me, "they may be planning to enact it quite literally. A vessel is required for the ceremony. A willing sacrifice—or perhaps just one that can't object."

My hands curled into fists. "I think it's Lady Miranda Fallon. All signs point to her. The cult used Isis to lure her in. Then the Osiris faction takes over, promising immortality, power, rebirth. But she will pay with her life."

Marlowe leaned forward, elbows on his knees. "Good Lord. Fallon's daughter can't be more than sixteen."

"Actually, she's seventeen. She fits the profile too well," I said quietly. "She was devastated by her father's death. Lady Fallon tried to help her deal with her grief as well as she could, but Miranda rebuked her mother's efforts. It was only when they traveled to Egypt that Miranda found a way. She grew fascinated by the god Osiris and the legend surrounding his resurrection. During a visit to the British Museum, she met a woman named Isis. We think she was the one who lured Miranda away from her home. I believe she will be the *Vessel* the Cult of Osiris will use to resurrect Osiris, as if such a thing could be done. That, of course, means she will be murdered."

"We need to act quickly," Robert said, his voice steel. "Ned, what did you find?"

My brother pushed back his damp hair and retrieved a folded piece of paper. "After gathering a list of antiquities shops from our list of clients, I visited nearly all of them. Most shop owners are charlatans. But three are legitimate—and one in particular stood out. Shopkeeper's name is Jasper Al-Masri. Half-Egyptian, half-British. Enthralled by the cult of Osiris. The man's got more scarabs than sense and claims to possess fragments of the Book of the Dead. He's also sold multiple items to Lord Greyston."

Marlowe sat up straighter. "Greyston? That odd fish? Dresses like a Turkish ambassador and drinks nothing but cinnamon liqueur? I know him."

Robert looked sharply at Ned. "That same shop—Al-Masri's—came up in Hassan's dealings, according to the information collected by Scotland Yard. The ledgers in Hassan's office list transactions with Al-Masri dating back six months. And even more concerning, he'd recently purchased embalming tools. Genuine, not replicas."

"Well, that explains the source of those tools in Hassan's office," I said. "No doubt about it. Henderson's murder and mummification, such as it was, was carried out there."

"Exactly," Robert said grimly. "Hassan must have worked with him, maybe as a go-between. Once Henderson was mummified, the cult no longer needed him. His death suggests the cult is tying off loose ends."

The phone rang in the hallway, jolting me. I'd given the

medium's assistant the residence phone number rather than the one in the parlor. It had to be her. I rushed to answer it. "Catherine Marsh speaking."

"Miss Marsh, this is Madame LeClair's assistant. It seems we have an opening. Our client canceled tonight's session. Madame LeClair can conduct a séance tonight. Say eight?"

"Yes, thank you. I'll be there."

"We'll see you then." The assistant ended the call.

As I stepped back into the library, everyone gazed at me with a question in their eyes.

"Madame LeClair's has had a cancellation. She can conduct a séance tonight."

"That's wonderful," Mellie said. "Maybe we'll get some answers."

Robert brushed a hand across his brow, his expression thoughtful. "There might be a problem, Catherine."

"Only one?" I teased gently, a soft smile tugging at my lips. "We must be having a good day."

He returned my smile, though his concern lingered. "As well-known as you are, you might be recognized."

I let out a quiet laugh. "I suppose that's the risk of being a woman of mystery and excellent taste." I patted his hand. "But you need not worry. Mellie and I have already thought this through. We will be heavily disguised. So will Ned." I turned to my brother. "Hopefully, you are free."

"I don't have anything planned." He didn't appear too thrilled about it.

"Mellie and I will be wearing dark frumpy gowns, hats, veils, the works, so we can blend in. Ned, you'll need to disguise yourself. As a gigolo."

Marlowe barked out a laugh. "Can't quite see that."

"Neither do I," Ned said in a doubting tone.

They had a point. Ned was the very image of a buttoned-down man.

"Consider it a compliment, Ned," Mellie said. "You are, after all, a handsome gentleman."

Ned's brow took a hike. "Marlowe would be a better choice."

"Oh, no. Not me. I wouldn't be able to keep a straight face."

"What about Robert?" Ned suggested. "He is your husband, Kitty."

"He's too well known. His face has been all over the newspapers for the last month, ever since . . . Never mind. It must be you, Ned."

"Very well."

"Hudson can fit you out, old bean," Robert said. "He's a wonder with costumes."

"If you say so. What would be my role in this?"

Mellie and I explained it to him.

"Let's hope Lily doesn't find out."

"I don't see why she would," Mellie said, a glint in her eye. "It's only for tonight."

"Ummm. Wouldn't Lady Emma be a better choice for the cousin?" he suggested.

"I'm beginning to feel insulted, Ned," Mellie said.

"It's not anything personally. It's just . . . you are young, and Lady Emma—"

"—Is an old crone?" Emma laughed.

Marlowe raised Emma's hand to his lips. "She can't attend the seance. She's helping me with Greyston. We'll reconnoiter tonight."

"Where?" Emma asked, her curiosity piqued.

Marlowe grinned. "Let's just say your gentleman's disguise will be of use."

She smiled back.

Robert tapped the table to get everyone's attention. "If we could get back to the business at hand?"

"Yes, of course, dear," I said, batting my eyelashes at him.

His lips briefly quirked before he made his point. "I'll explore Al-Masri's shop tonight. If there's something hidden there, I'll find it. We'll reconvene tomorrow afternoon."

"Can we make it tomorrow morning, say eleven?" I suggested. "I don't think we can wait until the afternoon."

There was a pause, the weight of our task settling over all of us like the storm outside.

"If the resurrection ritual is real—and it's happening soon —we may not get a second chance. We must move as quickly as we can."

Mellie's brow furrowed. "Larchmont said the stars must align. The Osiris ceremony relies on specific lunar patterns. The next ideal date is within the week."

A chill swept through me. "We have four days at most."

"Tomorrow at eleven it is," Ned said. Everyone agreed.

Emma and Marlowe wasted no time departing. I didn't blame them for their quick exit. They'd spent their day traveling only to take on an assignment that would more than likely last half the night. They needed all the rest they could get.

Ned offered to drive Mellie to Worthington House so she could rest. He would pick her and me up before heading off to the seance tonight.

Once they'd gone, Robert squeezed my hand, his touch brief but grounding. "It will work out, you'll see."

"I hope so." Eager for a moment of contemplation, I strolled toward the floor-to-ceiling window and watched the city blur behind the glass. I didn't know how I would stop a murder dressed up as a resurrection ritual. But whatever this cult had planned for Lady Miranda, they would not succeed.

Not if I had anything to say about it.

CHAPTER 15

WHISPERS FROM THE VEIL

*W*e arrived just after twilight, the sky bruised to a vengeful shade of purple, as if the heavens themselves had been struck. Fog slithered along the cobbles of Bloomsbury like a predator, thick and low, curling around our ankles with cold, damp fingers. The air was sodden with coal smoke and tension. Before us loomed the townhouse—tall, narrow, silent—a mausoleum dressed in velvet shadows. A small brass plaque, burnished by age and gleaming faintly beneath the gas lamp's flicker, read: *Madame LeClair, Spiritualist and Medium.* The letters curled like smoke, like secrets.

Ned adjusted his gloves with a flick that belied his unease, the knot of his ascot rakishly undone. He cast a sideways glance at Mellie and me. "Are you both *absolutely* certain I don't look like a lunatic?"

"You look like a rogue who seduces grieving widows out of their fortunes," Mellie replied, tugging her veil lower over her pale face. "Which, tonight, is precisely the impression we want."

My own disguise as Catherine Marsh was a shroud more than a costume. A black gown draped over me like mourning itself, my hair hidden beneath a dark wig and a wide-brimmed hat heavy with netting. My skin, powdered to near-corpse pallor, felt foreign to me. Beside me, Mellie—now Melissa Marsh—was the image of theatrical sorrow: skin ghostly pale, her eyes ringed with shadows, and a heavy scent of violet water and ancient incense clinging to her like the perfume of death. We looked like two cousins in mourning—or revenants escaped from a gothic tale.

The door creaked open, slow and ominous. A woman stood on the threshold—hollow-cheeked, with skin stretched tight and eyes so pale they looked carved from ice. She did not speak. She only beckoned, wordlessly, into the darkness.

The corridor was thick with velvet drapery, dimly lit by hissing gas sconces that cast our shadows long and trembling along the walls. The air hung heavy—beeswax and sandal-wood mingled with the faint, unmistakable tang of some-thing spoiled. Decay. Somewhere deeper in the townhouse, I heard a distant chime, the murmur of voices, and beneath it all . . . a sound like breath echoing from stone.

We were led into a chamber that felt less like a room and more like a tomb. Round, cloaked in darkness, the space seemed to pulse with warmth that felt wrong—like the heat of something buried. The windows were drowned in fabric. A black cat sat in one corner, watching, observing, not moving. In the center stood a round table draped in black velvet. Atop it, a single candle flickered in a crystal holder, its trembling flame casting spectral shadows that danced like the dead along the walls.

"Please," the assistant murmured, her voice like dry silk. "Take your seats. Madame LeClair will be with you shortly."

Even as she spoke, a shape moved in the shadows. Madame LeClair appeared without sound—gliding rather than walking, tall and statuesque, a creature not quite real. Her olive skin shimmered in the candlelight, her dark hair coiled into a Grecian knot, and her robe—silver, fluid—clung to her as if alive. Her eyes, dark and sharp as obsidian, swept over us with deliberate slowness.

She knew. Instantly, irrevocably. She *knew* we were lying.

As we introduced ourselves and our roles in this farce, she said nothing. Only allowed a faint, knowing smile to play at her lips—equal parts amusement and warning.

I took my seat between Mellie and Ned, whose jaw was clenched like stone. The silence pressed around us, intimate and suffocating, broken only by the hiss of incense being lit.

Sandalwood smoke curled into the air, veiling the room in shifting haze. The gaslights dimmed, swallowed by creeping shadow. The chamber shrank around us, the air tightening like a noose.

"Join hands," Madame LeClair commanded, her voice soft as a caress, cold as a blade. "Close your eyes. Breathe. Open yourselves to the unseen."

Our hands clasped. The candle flame trembled. A sudden gust—no breeze, no open window—brushed against my cheek, ice-cold and crawling. The flame sputtered violently, its light stuttering.

Then—she spoke.

But it was no longer Madame LeClair's voice.

The sound that issued from her lips was raw, rasping, guttural. It dragged through the room like iron chains on wet stone. My spine stiffened, my heart a thunderclap in my chest.

"There is unrest," the voice rasped, ancient and cruel.

A gasp—Mellie's, maybe mine—broke the silence.

"There is one among you who speaks not from grief . . . but from *deception*."

The words struck like a blow. I froze, blood pounding in my ears. Mellie's hand tightened around mine.

"Catherine Marsh," the voice sneered. "You seek a woman who loved you. A second mother. Vivienne."

The name sliced through me like a blade of ice. My breath hitched.

"You ask where she hid her will. But she did not summon you. She is not here."

I flinched. Cold dread spiraled in my chest, thick and choking.

Madame LeClair's head lolled. Her eyes fluttered open— pale, glowing, *inhuman*.

"But even false hearts draw true spirits," the voice said, softer now, with a mournful weight. "There is danger. Not for you . . . but for the one they call *The Vessel*."

The word struck the air like thunder.

"She is being prepared. She walks, blindfolded, toward the altar. The blood of Isis stains her fate. The chant will rise . . . and she will . . . fall."

The candle flickered again. I couldn't breathe.

"When?" Mellie whispered, her voice raw.

"When the moon is high. When the veil is thinnest. Four nights hence. Beneath stone. Beneath stars."

I shuddered. Four nights.

"The Osirion gathers. The girl must not ascend. Or the darkness shall."

With a violent shudder, Madame LeClair sat bolt upright. The candle blew out in a breathless gust. Total silence consumed the room.

Then, in her own shaken voice, she whispered, "The spirits have gone. They do not linger when darkness draws near."

Her gaze snapped to me—sharp, accusatory. "You are not Catherine Marsh."

"No," I admitted, trembling. "But I mean no harm. Please . . . you may have just saved someone's life."

Her eyes held mine. Burning. Measuring. "Then act swiftly. The Osirion has awakened."

"You speak of the Cult of Osiris."

Her mouth twisted. "I once laughed at them. Until a man in a golden mask came to me. He asked if I could summon the gods. He offered me gold. Power. I refused." She leaned closer. "But others did not."

"Who was he?"

"He didn't reveal himself."

"We believe the *Vessel* is Lady Miranda Fallon," I said.

Her face turned grave. "Then guard her well. They do not want secrecy anymore. They want spectacle. They want awe. And they especially want *blood*."

We left soon after, the fog outside thicker, clinging to us like ghostly hands. Coal smoke clung to our clothes, but beneath it—something else. Something older. Something *waiting*.

Ned didn't speak until we turned the corner.

"Well," he muttered. "That was bracing."

"Four nights," I whispered. "We have four nights to stop the resurrection rite."

"Beneath stone. Beneath stars," Mellie echoed. "A tomb? A crypt?"

"Or something made to look ancient," I said. "We need to search Greyston's holdings. Anything that could be used as an altar."

"And the golden mask?" she asked.

"I saw it," I said grimly. "In Larchmont's books. The High Priest of Osiris wore it."

Ned's voice was low. "That's who we need to find. The

one in the mask. The ceremony can't be conducted without him."

But the shadows of London were long . . . and masks, I feared, could hide any face. As the moon slipped behind the clouds above us, I knew. We weren't racing toward the truth.

We were racing toward a *sacrifice*.

CHAPTER 16

*T*he following morning, the investigative committee
gathered once more in our library. While a fresh
fire crackled in the hearth, the scent of strong coffee infused
the air, both providing a sense of comfort to a situation
which seemed dire in the extreme.

I'd barely slept. Dreams of shadowy figures cloaked in
linen and chanting in forgotten tongues had plagued my rest.
The others, bleary-eyed as they were, seemed just as
exhausted. But if their presence was anything to go by, they
were determined to get to the truth. We couldn't afford to
fail. More than one life hung in the balance.

"Thank you all for coming," I said softly, glancing from
face to weary face. "I know how tired you must be."

"No need to thank us, Kitty," Ned said. "We can rest after
we're done."

"Indeed," Mellie agreed.

"Then let us begin. Last night, Mellie, Ned, and I visited Madame LeClair's salon under our assumed names— Catherine and Melissa Marsh. Ned posed as Mellie's suitor."

"And aforementioned gigolo," Ned murmured.

Mellie shot him an amused look over her teacup. "You were splendid, Ned. I think you missed your calling."

"Heaven forbid," Ned retorted with a look of horror.

"The seance did not go quite according to plan," I continued, "Madame LeClair knew I was lying about my attempt to contact my dearly departed Aunt Vivienne regarding a missing will. She didn't scold me. Didn't even flinch. Instead, she told us something far more chilling.

Everyone leaned in. The silence that followed felt sacred, suspended.

"She said a ceremony was coming in four days. A vessel was to be sacrificed—willingly. To restore the power of the Osirion."

The air changed. The fire still crackled, but even it seemed quieter, like it too was listening.

Robert's voice was a low rumble. "Did she say where this ceremony might take place?"

"Under the moon. Under the stars," I answered.

"Well, that clears that right up," Marlowe scoffed. "Could be Hyde Park or a blasted field in Surrey."

She wasn't lying," I said. "Or if she was, it was the most convincing performance I've ever seen. Her eyes . . . her voice . . . there was something otherworldly about it."

"She made my skin crawl," Mellie said, visibly shivering. "The incense. That beast of a cat. And her eyes—they *glowed*, Kitty."

"A trick of the candlelight, surely," Ned said, though even he didn't sound convinced. "What matters is, she believes this. This cult, this Osirion—they're not just dressing up in robes for dramatic effect. They're seeking actual power. Resurrection."

Emma's eyes narrowed. "But how did she come by this knowledge? Don't tell me she spoke to Osiris himself."

"She was approached by a man in a gold mask who asked if she could summon gods. He offered her gold, power, but she refused. She sensed the darkness in him."

"I don't suppose she managed to learn his identity?" Robert asked.

"He was disguised."

"Anything else?" Robert asked.

"No. That's all." It didn't amount to much, but at least we'd learned the ceremony was to take place in four days. Well, three days now. "Did you learn anything?"

"I did," Opening the leather folio he'd brought with him, Robert withdrew several sheets of parchment and a slim, battered ledger. "Yesterday, I visited the shop of Jasper Al-Masri. He's vanished, but what he left behind was rather enlightening."

Placing the ledger on the round table, he beckoned us closer. "See?" He pointed to a column marked in tight Arabic script. "This is a list of names and corresponding deliveries—artifacts, ritual tools, books, and in one case, a box simply marked *Essence of Set*."

"What or who is Set?" I asked.

"The Egyptian god of chaos, storms, and the desert," Robert replied. "Feared and revered. The one who murdered Osiris."

"How did you know that?" I asked.

"I researched it after I arrived home." He pointed to a bookshelf stacked with scholarly tomes.

"Clever you," I said.

Offering me a soft smile, he continued, "It's not the

contents that interested me most, but the recipients. Several names repeat. One address in particular appears five times."

"Let me guess," I said, already feeling my stomach twist. "Lord Greyston?"

Robert nodded. "He was not merely dabbling. He was actively involved. One of the entries includes the word *tahut*, which means *ritual leader* in ancient Egyptian."

"Well, that tracks," Ned said.

Robert continued, "The final entry, dated a week ago, reads: *Items delivered. Ceremony imminent. All in place.*"

Marlowe straightened up. "That aligns with what Emma and I found."

His intended cast him a look. "You *found* a cigar and a card game. I did the actual sleuthing."

Marlowe grinned unrepentantly. "Touché."

Emma turned her attention to the group. "Greyston was at the Lamb's Eye Gentlemen's Club last night. Nothing overtly sinister—he was gambling, drinking, being perfectly aristocratic. I made my way through the room, dressed as a young man, of course, which worked well—"

"—until it didn't," Marlowe interjected. "Two gentlemen took a shine to our young rake."

Emma hitched up her chin. "Not my fault I'm devastating in a waistcoat."

"You're devastating in whatever you wear, my dear," Marlowe said, pressing a kiss to her hand.

I smiled despite myself. "Did you manage to gather anything useful in between rebuffing proposals?"

"I did. There were whispers—one man said Greyston was 'finally going through with it.' Another mentioned fire rites. And something about 'the eye being opened.' It wasn't a secret, Kitty. Not among them. They *know* something is coming."

Robert frowned. "Did anyone mention a date?"

"No," Emma said. "But they spoke like it was happening soon. Very soon."

I exhaled slowly. "That confirms what Madame LeClair said. We're nearly out of time." As the fire popped in the grate, everyone seemed to feel the shift as though sensing something dark drawing near. "The cult needs three things. A high priest, a sacred place, and a vessel. Willing. Human."

Robert solemnly nodded. "And given Madame LeClair's comment, they already have one."

The silence that followed was unbearable.

"So, what now?" Marlowe interjected. We have a name— Greyston—and an idea of what they're planning. But do we stop him now and risk tipping our hand, or wait until he leads us to the site?"

"We can't wait," I said. "Lady Miranda could already be in danger. And there might be more than one so-called vessel. Who's to say they don't have another one in case the first ceremony fails? What's to stop them from going further than even they intended?"

Robert's eyes met mine. Steady. Unyielding. "We need proof. Solid, irrefutable proof."

"Then we follow the ledger," Ned said, standing. "Visit the addresses this afternoon. Speak to anyone Jasper sold to. If they're involved, we'll know it. If they're victims, they may need help."

"Marlowe and I can take the west end," Emma offered. "We can pose as collectors interested in ritual pieces."

"I'll take the Bloomsbury leads," Mellie said, reaching for the ledger.

"Not alone, you won't," Ned said. "Hollingsworth would have our guts for garters if anything happened to you. You've already had one close call."

Mellie's chin came up. "I can manage, Ned."

"You're an innocent, Mellie. That's what they want. What's to say they won't pressure you to act as a vessel?"

"I wouldn't. It does have to be voluntary."

"They will drug you first. Once they do that, you will agree to anything."

Mellie faltered. "Umm, well, you do have a point."

"I'll pay another visit to Madame LeClair," I said. "Alone, this time. I want to know more about this ceremony. She might not know the identity of the man in the gold mask. But she might know more about the ritual. Any information, no matter how small, might provide a clue to its location."

Robert's jaw clenched. "Not by yourself."

I reached across the table and laced my fingers with his. "With you nearby, then."

The committee, ragtag and extraordinary, began to shift —assignments in hand, tension thick in the air. But as I gathered my notes, I felt something hard and unrelenting in my chest. We were drawing closer to the truth, yes—but closer, too, to whatever darkness waited beneath it.

Just as Robert closed the ledger, the library door burst open.

Julian Banks stood in the doorway, chest heaving, collar askew, hair windblown, his face white with urgency.

Behind him, our butler sputtered indignantly. "Lord Rutledge—Lady Rutledge—I tried to stop this gentleman, but—"

"It's fine, Mister Black," I said, stepping forward. "I know Mister Banks."

Julian looked at me, eyes wild. "Forgive the intrusion, but there's something you need to know."

"What happened?" Robert demanded.

"Professor Larchmont has been attacked."

CHAPTER 17

BLOODLINES AND BETRAYALS

*T*he air seemed to vanish from the room.

"When? What happened?" I asked, already striding toward Julian, dread slamming into me like a wave.

"Sometime this morning. His housekeeper found him on the fourth-floor landing, barely conscious. I arrived just as he was being loaded into an ambulance. He'd been struck on the head—blunt force. He surprised someone in the act of robbing him."

"Dear heaven," Mellie murmured, clutching the back of a chair.

"Was he conscious?" Robert asked. "Could he speak?"

"He was drifting in and out," Julian replied, his face etched with worry. "But that's not the worst of it."

I felt the blood drain from my face.

"They stole the *Book of the Dead*," Julian said, his voice dropping to a near whisper. "The one with the annotations. Larchmont's copy."

The room was utterly still.

"His collection was ransacked," Julian continued, striding farther into the room, the urgency in his movements matching the dread rising in my chest. "As far as I could see, that book was the only thing taken. They knew exactly what they wanted."

Robert turned to me. "I'll send word to Scotland Yard. We need officers at Larchmont's townhouse. Who's to say they won't return?"

I turned to Julian. "Did the housekeeper see anyone? Anything?"

"She was downstairs at the time and didn't hear a thing. But the professor's cat—Anubis—was acting strange all morning. Hissing at corners. Bolting from shadows." He shook his head. "I know it sounds absurd, but I think he witnessed the attack."

"I don't think it sounds absurd at all," I said softly. "If they have the *Book of the Dead*, and the ceremony is imminent— then it's not just speculation anymore. They mean to go through with it."

Ned stepped forward; his voice clipped. "What exactly does this book contain?"

"Ritual instructions," Julian answered. "Spells. Incantations. Descriptions of how the soul journeys through the afterlife. Larchmont believed this copy contained annotations that described how to reenact the rites of Osiris. He didn't think it was symbolic. He thought it was a *manual*."

"And now it's in the hands of madmen," Emma muttered.

"Or worse," Mellie said, eyes wide. "Believers."

I pressed my hand to my stomach, trying to still the sick churn. Gentle and dithery Larchmont had been the only one who truly understood what we were up against. And now he'd nearly been killed for it.

"They're accelerating their plans," Robert said. "Possibly out of fear. We've been asking too many questions. Pressing too close."

"So, what now?" Ned asked, frustration simmering beneath his words.

"We reformulate our plans," Robert said before turning to Julian. "Mister Banks, I'm Robert Crawford Sinclair, Catherine's husband. Some know me as Lord Rutledge." Pointing to the other members of the committee, he introduced them in turn. "Ned Worthington, Catherine's brother, Lord Marlowe, and Lady Emma. Mellie, you know."

Julian gave a curt nod. "Pleased to meet all of you. Please call me Julian."

"Julian, it is," Robert said. "I want you to stay with Catherine. The two of you know Larchmont's notes better than any of us. Go back to his house, go through anything that might give us the location of the ceremony. A church, a tomb, a crypt—somewhere ancient and hidden. It's vital we find the location."

Emma stepped forward. "And Marlowe and I?"

"Greyston's activities need to be monitored. I'll contact Peters. He assisted with the Mistletoe Shoppe investigation. He's very discreet. The three of you will need to keep a watch on him. He'll need to be shadowed day and night. Do you think that's something you could manage?"

Marlowe nodded. "Whatever it takes."

"Absolutely," Emma echoed.

"And me?" Ned asked.

Robert handed him the ledger. "Visit the addresses we discussed earlier. Speak to those involved in the deliveries. Pretend to be Al-Masri's apprentice, his partner, I don't care —just get us more names. Take Mellie with you."

"What about Larchmont's study?" Mellie asked, her voice

tight with determination. "Shouldn't I direct my efforts there?"

Robert turned to her, his expression shadowed with worry. "Whoever attacked Larchmont might return. I won't risk your life, Mellie."

"But Kitty's going!" she cried, a flash of indignation in her eyes.

"Catherine can defend herself," he said quietly, but with unshakable certainty.

A warmth spread through my chest, fierce and sudden. He believed in me. Not just as a wife—but as someone who could stand her ground.

Robert stepped closer to Mellie and gently rested his hands on her shoulders. "I know you're capable. And I know how much you want to help. But a good soldier chooses the path that serves the greater good. Go with Ned. Keep your eyes and ears open. So, nothing catches us off guard."

Mellie hesitated; her lips pressed into a firm line. Then, with a reluctant nod, she exhaled. "Very well."

The fire in her voice had dimmed—but had not gone out.

"We need to find Isis," I said, my voice low but firm. "She's the key. Without her, the ritual can't be completed."

Julian frowned. "You don't think the medium was Isis?"

I shook my head and launched into a breathless account of everything that had happened the night before—Madame LeClair's cryptic words, the altar, the terrifying glimpse into what was to come.

When I finished, Julian leaned in. "Describe her."

"Dark hair, olive skin—"

"No," he interrupted sharply. "It's not her. The woman I saw at the British Museum was blonde. Strikingly beautiful. Impossible to forget."

A cold jolt shot through me. I stiffened. "Tall?" I asked, already fearing the answer. "Eyes like sapphires?"

Julian nodded. "Yes. How did you—?"

My breath caught. No. No, it couldn't be her. Not *her*.

"Lady Fallon," Marlowe said grimly, his voice slicing through the silence like a blade.

Mellie went ghost-pale. "But—Miranda's her daughter."

"Not by blood," Emma said quietly, her eyes narrowing. "Or so the whispers went."

Of course, Emma would know. She was attuned to the noble grapevine like a cat to a canary cage—an unfortunate byproduct of being Lady Carlyle's daughter. There wasn't a single scandal, affair, or illegitimate child she hadn't heard about by the second course of supper.

I turned to her, heart pounding. "What do you mean, Emma?"

"Lord Fallon was a confirmed bachelor. Not an unusual thing for a middle-aged peer. Plenty of time to marry and beget an heir. He kept a mistress whom, by all accounts, he truly loved. But marriage was out of the question. She was hardly the sort of female a baron took to wife. And then out of the blue, he married the woman we know as Lady Fallon and took her for an extended honeymoon to parts unknown. A year later, they returned to England with a babe in tow— Miranda. Rumors ran rampant about the legitimacy of the child. Some claimed his mistress was the true mother. Apparently, she'd disappeared and was never seen again. No one disputed Miranda's birth to Lord Fallon, of course, and Lady Fallon never whispered a word."

"Even if Lady Fallon is not Miranda's natural mother, that wouldn't stop her from loving her," Mellie said. "Children are usually treasured by their adoptive mothers."

"But this was a different situation," Emma explained. "Miranda would have been forced on her. More than likely, Lord Fallon made that a requirement of the marriage. She would have agreed to anything to lift herself out of poverty."

"Poverty?" I asked.

"Lady Fallon's family was destitute. Her father, the second son of a second son of a viscount, inherited none of the family's wealth. As an educated man, he was able to gain employment as a law clerk. His wages were barely enough to keep his family fed, clothed, and housed. But when he died, his wife and daughter were reduced to doing menial work—laundry, sewing, whatever tasks earned them enough money to keep them from roaming the streets. I have no idea how Lord Fallon found her. I'd have to ask Mama about that. But somehow, he did. He must have offered her marriage to legitimize his child. She agreed to it, probably hoping she'd have a babe of her own."

"She didn't have a child, though," I said.

"No."

"How on earth did she manage to keep that magnificent mansion—and the fortune required to run it?" I asked, still marveling. "Shouldn't it have passed to the next male heir?"

"Miranda *is* the heir," came the reply. "In fact, *she* is Lady Fallon. The title belongs to her."

Marlowe scoffed. "Impossible. Women can't inherit titles."

"In most cases, no," Emma replied smoothly. "But the Fallon title is an exception. It's one of the oldest in England—13th century, if memory serves. It was established as a barony by writ, not by patent. That means it doesn't pass strictly down the male line. If there's no son, a daughter may inherit both the title and the estate."

"So, Miranda holds the title outright?" I asked.

"Yes. And because the title was created under the barony of writ, she can assign the Fallon property as she sees fit. Lady Fallon cannot be awarded the title, but she can inherit the property. Miranda would have to will the Fallon property, which is extensive, to her mother."

"But she's only seventeen," I said. "Can she legally do that?"

"Not until her eighteenth birthday."

"That's two days from now. Lady Fallon mentioned it when she showed me Miranda's miniature." Suddenly, the Machiavellian scheme became crystal clear. "That's why Miranda is the *Vessel*. So, Lady Fallon can inherit the entire fortune."

"That's beyond evil," Lady Mellie said. "That's downright monstrous."

"Before we continue down this road," Ned said, "may I remind you we don't have a shred of evidence that Lady Fallon is in fact Isis."

"Well, that can be easily ascertained," I said. "We'll arrange for her to meet Julian."

"When?"

"Today." I turned to Julian. "Are you game?"

"Need you ask? I'll do anything to save that young woman from certain death and hopefully avenge the damage done to Professor Larchmont."

"So, given Julian's news, how should we proceed?" Mellie asked, her voice taut with urgency.

"Lord Greyston still needs to be watched," Marlowe said grimly. "That hasn't changed."

Robert gave a curt nod. "I'll telephone Peters. Have him reach out to you within the hour. You'll be at home, I presume?"

Marlowe nodded. "So will Emma. She's measuring for new curtains."

"I am *not!*" Emma huffed, swatting his arm. "You've a beautiful home, Marlowe. I wouldn't change a single thing."

"You say that now," he teased, eyes gleaming. "But once you're Lady Marlowe? Who knows what chaos you'll unleash."

A ripple of laughter circled the room, except for Ned.

Robert noticed first. "What's wrong?"

"We're no closer to finding out who murdered Henderson," Ned said, voice low. "And time's slipping through our fingers."

A heavy silence settled over us.

"We will," I said firmly. "It's all connected, Ned. Every path—every strange clue—it all leads back to the same place."

He looked away. "It'll break Mother's heart if we fail."

I reached across the space between us, wrapping my fingers around his. "We won't. I promise you."

His hand tightened in mine, but doubt still clouded his eyes. "If you say so . . ."

"What about you, Robert?" I asked, needing something to cling to.

"I'm going back to the British Museum. I want a word with the director."

"He won't see you," I said softly.

Robert's eyes darkened with purpose. "He may turn away Chief Detective Inspector Robert Crawford Sinclair, but he won't dare refuse the Marquis of Rutledge. Especially not one who's just about to fund the restoration of three priceless sarcophagi."

"Bribery, my dear?" I asked, forcing a smile.

"Persuasion," he countered. "It's an ancient and subtle art."

"And what do you hope to find?"

"Answers," he said. "The director knew Henderson well. If Henderson was involved or knew something, it might be hidden in his office. Notes, maps, symbols. Anything that would tell us where this ceremony is taking place."

I tried to hold on to the flicker of hope his words offered, but my heart felt like it had turned to lead. A storm was brewing—darker, more dangerous than anything we'd faced before.

The Osirion no longer lurked in shadows. They had what they needed to unleash whatever horror they had planned.

We had to stop them.

Before Miranda's eighteenth birthday became her last.

CHAPTER 18

THE HOLLOW SMILE

*W*e didn't wait for an invitation. In matters of life—or the defilement of death—hesitation could mean the difference between salvation and ruin.

Julian and I ascended the front steps of the Fallon townhouse, our footsteps striking sharply and purposefully against the pale stone. The butler opened the door with a flicker of surprise that quickly hardened into caution. We must have looked grave—because we were.

"We have urgent news for Lady Fallon," I said, channeling every ounce of authority I could summon as Lady Rutledge. "It concerns her daughter. Please inform her that we must speak with her immediately."

The butler hesitated only a beat before bowing and disappearing down the corridor like a shadow on command. I turned to Julian, my heart pounding against my ribs. The air around this place felt colder than it should, like rot just beneath the surface. I didn't want to be here. But Miranda was in danger—and that mattered more than fear.

"She'll see us," I whispered. "If she's involved—if she knows what's coming—she won't be able to help herself."

Julian gave a tight nod. "And if we're lucky, she'll lead us straight to the heart of it."

The butler reappeared without a word and gestured us inside. As I crossed the threshold, I felt it—a hush. Thick and unnatural, like the silence before a ritual begins.

We weren't shown to the same room as before. This drawing room was pristine—eerily so. Pale blue wallpaper, silver accents, a fire flickering low in the hearth, too low to warm, too perfect to be accidental. It was staged—*presented*—like a place where truth never lived.

Lady Fallon stood at the window in a gown the color of winter fog, her presence as immaculate and hollow as carved marble. The scent of roses clung to her like a mask. She turned, smiling with an elegance that didn't touch her eyes.

"Lady Rutledge. What an unexpected pleasure," she said, voice smooth as silk.

Not a single word of it felt real.

"May I present Lord Greyston and Mr. Fadil Amin?" she added, gesturing toward the men beside her.

Greyston wore the finery Marlowe had described—embroidered vestments in the Ottoman style, his expression cool and predatory. Fadil Amin I recognized from Robert's ledgers, though I'd never met him. My pulse surged. Ceremonial oils. Embalming agents. Linen wrappings. All of them traced back to him.

I smiled politely. "A pleasure."

Julian echoed the sentiment, but I could feel his unease radiating like heat.

"I apologize for the intrusion," I said, eyes returning to

Lady Fallon. "We've come across something delicate concerning your daughter. Might we speak in private?"

A flicker of emotion passed over her face—not fear. Not surprise. Something colder. Calculation. Still, she nodded. "Of course."

She led us down the corridor to a smaller parlor—sunlit and softly appointed, but with the same curated stillness. This was a room for secrets, confessions. And perhaps, for lies.

"What is it?" she asked, once the door clicked shut.

I drew in a breath, steadying myself. "We believe Miranda is in danger."

Her eyes widened slightly—just enough to feign concern. Not enough to feel it.

"There are people," I went on, "planning a resurrection ritual rooted in Osirian rites. They believe Miranda is the *The Vessel*. The key."

Lady Fallon placed a gloved hand to her chest with theatrical grace. "This is preposterous."

"We have evidence," Julian said quietly. "Professor Larchmont, an Egyptian scholar, was attacked this morning. His annotated *Book of the Dead*—detailing the rite—was stolen."

She didn't gasp. Didn't flinch. She simply blinked once.

I leaned in. "You're her mother. I thought you should know. There's still time to protect her."

A long, dreadful pause followed. Then, that same soft, unreadable smile.

"Thank you," she said, the words cool as cut glass. "I'll speak to my new investigator. He'll look into it and find Miranda."

And just like that, we were dismissed.

Escorted once again by the silent butler, the front door closed behind us with the weight of stone.

Julian and I stood motionless on the front steps, the wind sharp against our faces.

"It's her," I said quietly. "Isn't it? Isis. The woman you saw."

"Yes." The certainty in his voice sent a chill down my spine. "There's no doubt."

"She didn't ask a single question," I whispered. "Not why, Miranda. Not how we knew. She already knew."

"Yes. That was rather odd."

"But not unexpected," I said, my jaw clenched.

"What do we do now?" Julian asked.

"We wait. We follow. Let's see what Lady Fallon does when no one's watching."

We crossed the street and ducked beneath the shade of an old chestnut tree. I clenched my fists until my knuckles ached. Minutes crawled by.

Then—the door opened.

Lady Fallon emerged, moving with swift, deliberate grace. Fadil Amin followed like a shadow. Greyston was last, unreadable as he handed her into a gleaming black Rolls Royce.

Once it disappeared, I shot up, waving my arms at a passing cab. "Taxi!"

When it screeched to a halt, I practically shoved Julian inside before leaping in myself.

"There's a black Rolls ahead," I told the driver, breathless. "Don't lose it—but stay back."

"Understood, Miss."

As the cab rumbled to life, my gaze never left the car ahead.

"They're going to the ritual site," Julian whispered low enough so the cabbie could not hear. "I just know it."

I nodded, the certainty settling like stone in my gut. "We're about to find out where."

The cab rumbled over cobbled streets, trailing the Rolls through winding roads away from Mayfair. I barely noticed the changing landscape—just the gleam of the car ahead, the tension simmering in my chest like a storm ready to break.

"They're accelerating everything," I murmured. "Miranda turns eighteen in two days. Once she signs over her inheritance—"

"They'll kill her," Julian said, voice like flint.

Finally, after what seemed forever, the Rolls turned down a narrow, private lane flanked by yew trees. The long, winding road led to an old ivy-covered chapel. Long since abandoned by God, it seemed.

A man in a dark robe opened the back door of the Rolls and bowed low as Lady Fallon stepped out.

Julian inhaled sharply. "I saw that man at the museum. At the reception."

I couldn't speak. My throat burned with fury. With grief.

Lady Fallon entered the chapel. A traitor to a daughter. About to sacrifice Miranda for a pot of gold.

"We found them," I whispered. "This is it."

Julian turned to me, his eyes blazing. "The others need to know."

"Yes, they do." Tonight, we'd finish this madness.

Before they spilled innocent blood.

Before they raised something that should remain buried forever.

CHAPTER 19

INTO THE TEMPLE'S SHADOW

"*T*hat will be a pound six shillings, Miss," the cab driver said, turning around.

"Get on with you!" Julian exclaimed, scandalized at the outrageous fare. "You're putting us on!"

"Julian, don't quibble," I said, digging into my handbag as I turned to the cabbie. "We're not done yet, my good man."

The cabbie touched his cap, "Yes, Miss."

As the Rolls Royce vanished behind the chapel, Julian and I remained crouched in the back seat. We were far enough away from the building that we couldn't be seen.

"One of us has to warn the others," I whispered, heart pounding. "I think it should be you."

Julian shot me a sharp look. "You're not seriously thinking of going in there alone."

"I am. You need to get back—tell Robert what we've found. He'll be at the British Museum."

"I'm not leaving you to walk into that place by yourself,"

he said, voice low and tight. "That woman is dangerous. And if she's who we think she is—if she's Isis—"

"She is," I cut in. "I know it. Every instinct in me is screaming it."

He clenched his jaw. "Then all the more reason I should stay."

I touched his arm. "Julian. You're brilliant. But let's be honest—you've never done any breaking and entering."

"And you have?"

"Twice. First time Robert arrested me."

He huffed in disbelief, but the corner of his mouth twitched.

"Listen to me. This is where the ceremony will be held. They can't hold it without Miranda. I can find her—and once I do, we'll hide until you return with help."

"Once you find her, where will you go?"

I pointed to the trees that surrounded us. "Into the woods. We'll hide until you return with help."

He stared at me for a long moment. Then he exhaled, resigned.

"You'd better find Miranda, Miss Worthington. And keep you both alive."

"I will."

I pressed two pounds into the cabbie's hand. "Julian will pay you another two—"

"That's highway robbery!" Julian muttered.

"It's money well spent." I turned to the cabbie. "You are to take him to the British Museum and anywhere else he needs to go. I promise you will be well compensated."

The cabbie's eyes flicked toward the chapel. "Is someone in danger? In there?" Seemingly, he'd heard at least part of our conversation.

"There is. A young woman, an innocent. If we don't stop

what they have planned for her, she will die. I'm depending on you."

"You can count on me, Miss," he said solemnly.

"Thank you." I handed Julian my handbag. "There's more money inside if you need it."

He nodded, his throat working.

Without another word, I slipped from the cab into the trees and watched as the taxicab disappeared from view.

I was alone.

Gravestones lined the side of the chapel, half-sunken and crooked with age. I crept toward the rear, keeping low. There —almost lost in the ivy—was a narrow side door. Old. Rusted. But recently oiled. My hand trembled as I pushed it open.

Slipping inside, the darkness swallowed me.

Not the gentle sort that comes with candlelight or dusk. But the heavy kind—thick, clinging, ancient. It smelled of wax and decay. A sickening scent that coiled through my nostrils and lodged in the back of my throat.

I paused to let my eyes adjust.

The space before me had once been a chapel proper. The pews were long gone. In their place, rows of low stools formed a circle around a black-draped altar. Symbols I couldn't read ringed the stone slab, smeared in something dark and dreadful. Blood. Or a gruesome imitation.

A pulse beat in the air. Low and deep, like something breathing beneath the surface. It pressed against my skin, against my chest. Something had happened here—would happen again. This was where they meant to kill her.

My stomach twisted as I circled the altar in silence, eyes flicking over unlit torches and puddles of wax. Candles. Offerings. Everything was prepared.

They couldn't hold the ceremony without the *Vessel*. And that meant I had to find Miranda.

I moved deeper, down a shadowy corridor lined with doors. I didn't need them all—I needed one. The one with Miranda.

Then I heard them.

Voices. Close.

Panicking, I slipped through the nearest door and pulled it shut behind me as footsteps approached.

I crouched in the dark, heart hammering against my ribs. My breathing impossibly loud. A key rattled somewhere down the hall.

Then silence.

I stood slowly, taking in the space.

It was a reliquary of horrors. Shelves of jars, vessels, and gleaming bronze tools. Scrolls, statues, skulls. A golden scarab caught the light, and beside it—an effigy. A woman bound at the wrists, carved in lifelike detail. A grotesque rehearsal for a living sacrifice.

Bile rose in my throat. I had to get out of here.

I gathered my courage and cracked open the door. The footsteps and voices had faded away. I carefully made my way out into the corridor. It was darker here—farther from the ceremonial chamber, the scent of incense and sandalwood slowly replaced by something more sinister: mildew, damp stone, the faint, coppery tang of fear. I moved with care, my gloved fingers brushing the cold stone wall as I searched for another passage, another clue. That was when I noticed it: a door, tucked behind a hanging tapestry of Isis offering her arms to Osiris. Fitting.

The door was bolted shut, the handle smooth from age, the keyhole worn but not immune to ingenuity.

I dropped to one knee, tugging a curved hairpin from beneath my hat. Robert would cheer at my ingenuity. He should. He'd taught me this trick.

I inserted the pin, feeling for the tumblers. One click. Two. A third. The lock gave with a soft, metallic sigh.

"Hello?" I whispered, stepping into the room.

It was dark, the only light a sliver filtering through a small, high window. Then, from the far corner, a rustle.

She was huddled there, half-curled against the wall like a wounded bird. Her gown—white and ceremonial—was torn and streaked with dust. Her hair, long and wild, clung to her cheeks. But her eyes—wide and frightened—were unmistakable.

"Miranda," I said gently, crouching beside her. "I'm Kitty Worthington. I'm here to help you."

She flinched. "Are you with my mother?"

"No," I whispered. "I'm the opposite of her. I'm here to get you out."

Tears welled in her eyes as she collapsed into me, trembling.

"She drugged me," she sobbed. "I thought I was coming to learn. But she . . . she hates me. I never understood why. I was never enough. Not clever enough, not obedient enough—"

"You don't have to explain," I said, pulling her to her feet. "We don't have time. We need to move. Now."

"They want to use me for a resurrection ritual. They say I'm pure. That I belong to the bloodline. Whatever that means. But I won't do it. I'd rather die." I didn't have the heart to tell her that was the plan.

"You won't be used," I promised. "Not while I'm here."

She was weak, barely able to stand. I suspected they'd been starving her, keeping her pliable. But she still had strength enough to stand, to walk. That would have to be enough. Together, we slipped out, retracing my path—left at the broken torch bracket, past the amphorae, toward the exit.

But then I heard it.

Voices. Footsteps. Chanting.

I peeked around the corner—and froze.

Half a dozen robed figures glided toward us, masks glinting in the flickering light. One, in gold, moved with unmistakable authority. Beneath that mask, I sensed a terrible familiarity.

Miranda tensed beside me. "That's him. That's the one who touches me after they drug me. Not . . . inappropriately. He said I must be kept pure."

Ice crawled down my spine.

"We have to go," I hissed. "Come. This way."

We ducked into the shadows, keeping low, dodging into shadows and side chambers as needed. Eventually, I found another corridor—narrow, cracked, the air smelling faintly of wet earth. At the end: a door, old and iron-bound.

It creaked open to reveal a sloping tunnel leading upward —and the woods beyond.

We didn't hesitate. We ran.

The air was cold. Too cold for Miranda, who gasped as the night wind touched her skin. She was barefoot, and her ceremonial dress offered little protection. I took off my coat and wrapped it around her shoulders.

We pressed on, the trees closing in around us. The path was thick with brambles and roots, and the light was fading fast.

"Why don't we take the lane that led to the chapel?" she asked, urgency in her voice.

"That's the first place they'll look once they realize you're missing. We must stick to the woods." Only then would we have a chance of escaping.

"How far to the road?" she asked.

"I don't know," I admitted. "But if we keep going, we'll find something. A farm. A cottage. Anything."

She nodded, teeth chattering. "They told me . . . if I

agreed, they'd feed me. Let me see the stars again. I haven't been outside in weeks. They were waiting for my birthday, I heard one of them say."

"Then we escaped just in time."

The forest thickened. Our pace slowed. The stars blinked through the canopy above, but they gave little comfort. Miranda stumbled more than once, and I had to half-carry her as we went. My own legs ached, and my skirts were heavy with dew and mud.

But then I heard it.

Low at first. Distant.

Then louder.

Dogs. Baying. Sniffing. Hunting.

My heart slammed into my ribs. "They're tracking us."

Miranda's eyes filled with terror. "They'll kill us."

"No, they won't," I said, my voice firmer than I felt. "Not if we stay ahead. Can you walk faster?"

"I'll try." Somehow, she dug deep, and her steps went from a walk to a run.

Branches lashed my face, twigs snapped beneath our feet. Behind us, the hounds howled louder, joined now by male voices shouting commands.

I risked a glance back—but the darkness swallowed everything.

Miranda stumbled again, and I caught her. "Just a bit farther. We'll find a road. A motorcar. A light in the distance."

"I can't," she whispered.

"You've made it this far, Miranda. Don't give up now."

We pressed on. I didn't know where I was going. I couldn't even be sure we weren't running in circles.

But I knew one thing with certainty:

We would not die in that forest.

Not tonight.

Not for some twisted version of resurrection.

Not while I still had breath in my lungs.

As the dogs closed in, I clutched Miranda's hand tighter, dragging her forward into the endless dark.

Branches clawed at our arms as we pushed deeper into the forest, each step slower than the last. Miranda stumbled again, falling to her knees with a faint cry. I dropped beside her, my chest heaving.

"I can't," she whispered. "I can't go on."

"You can," I urged, grabbing her arm. "Just a little farther. We have to keep moving."

She was freezing, barefoot, and starved. The dogs were nearly on us now, their howls echoing like ghosts through the trees. Closer. Closer.

I helped her to her feet, half-carrying her as we stumbled forward. The woods thickened again, closing in around us like a noose. I kept looking for a break in the trees, a glimmer of light—anything.

Then I heard it.

Not the baying of the hounds this time.

Voices.

Soft at first, then rising in chant. Low, rhythmic, unnatural. My blood turned to ice.

Miranda choked. "It's them."

We skidded to a halt, only to see figures emerging from the darkness all around us—hooded and robed in black and crimson, masks glinting with gold in the faint light of their lanterns.

We'd run right into them.

I turned, dragging Miranda back the way we'd come, but two more figures stepped from the trees behind us, blocking the path.

A man stepped forward; his face hidden behind a gleaming gold mask shaped like a falcon's head—Imhotep. The High Priest.

He raised a hand. "You should not have interfered, Miss Worthington."

I stepped in front of Miranda. "Let her go. She has nothing to do with you—"

"She has everything to do with us," he said, his voice calm. Certain. "She is *The Vessel*. The offering. The bridge."

"Then take me instead," I snapped. "Whatever this is—this madness—end it with me."

A faint chuckle rippled through the masked figures.

"You are clever," the priest said, stepping closer. "And brave. But this isn't something you can bargain with. The ritual is in motion. And now . . . you'll bear witness."

Rough hands seized my arms. Another cultist took Miranda, who whimpered, too weak to fight back. I struggled, kicked—but it was useless.

They dragged us through the trees, the chanting rising behind us like a tide. The golden mask glinted in the moonlight as the priest turned and led the way back toward the temple.

And just before we disappeared once more beneath the canopy of ancient trees, I looked up at the night sky—black and endless—and wondered if anyone would find us in time.

CHAPTER 20

THE GODDESS IN THE DARK

I awoke to cold.

A bone-deep, marrow-chilling cold that pressed into my skin and curled like fog in my lungs. I couldn't see anything—just blackness, thick and endless. The scent of damp stone and something sickly sweet hung in the air.

I shifted, and pain flared in my wrists.

My hands were tied.

Panic surged through me.

I was lying on a bed—high, unfamiliar, and plush beneath me in a way that felt more like a coffin than a comfort. I tried to sit up, but my body felt wrong. Slow. Ungoverned. My feet refused to obey, and my thoughts slid sideways, as though my mind had turned to syrup.

I'd been drugged.

They'd stripped me of my clothes, too. I was wearing a

robe—sleeveless, ceremonial. The cotton fabric clung to my skin like a shroud.

Miranda.

I bolted upright, despite the spinning in my head. "Miranda?"

No answer.

She wasn't here. I was alone.

A deep shiver passed through me—not from the cold this time, but from the certainty that I had failed. Miranda was gone. Taken. The ritual—

A loud click broke the silence.

The door swung open.

And in stepped Lady Fallon, an oil lantern in her hand.

She wore black. Not a plain one like mine, but fancier, silk embroidered with gold. Her blonde hair was coiled high on her head, a crown of twisted braids encircling her brow. Her lips were painted crimson, her eyes outlined like those of an ancient Egyptian queen. Her smile sent a chill through my very bones.

"Well," she said, stepping closer, her heels echoing ominously. "The offering awakens."

I didn't respond. My voice was still sluggish in my throat, but my glare was steady.

She circled the bed, her fingers trailing across the carved wood frame. "Do you like the gown? It was made especially for you. Well, for the offering. You walked into our trap. As I knew you would."

"Where is she?" I rasped.

"Miranda?" She gave a delicate laugh. "Safe and sound. For now."

My fists clenched against the restraints. "If you hurt her—"

"Oh, darling, I've been hurting her all her life." Lady

Fallon perched at the end of the bed, smoothing her robe with reverence, as if preparing to speak before an altar.

"I married a man twice my age," she began, eyes flickering with something between nostalgia and rage. "To escape poverty. My family had nothing left but debts and delusions of grandeur. So, I did what any clever woman would do—I secured my future. Or tried to."

Her lips curled. "What I didn't anticipate was that I wouldn't even be allowed to enjoy my husband's wealth. He withheld everything from me. Locked up the accounts. Monitored every step I took. I wasn't even allowed to leave the house without him. And when he traveled? I was brought along like a trained animal."

I said nothing, watching her closely.

"He married me for appearances only," she said. "Wouldn't touch me. Wouldn't give me a child. He had one already—his precious Miranda. The daughter of a whore. When the woman died in childbirth, he brought the girl to me. Told me I would play the part of mother. Raise her like my own. In exchange, I would be a lady, live in a mansion, wear beautiful clothes." Once more, she smoothed her hand over the silk. "But it wasn't enough. Not nearly enough."

Lady Fallon's eyes went cold. "I never wanted her. I tolerated her. Barely. Do you know what it's like to be treated like an ornament by a man, and then expected to raise his bastard as a penance? It curdles the soul. But I made him pay. By God, I did."

I swallowed hard as I realized what she'd done. "You killed him."

"Oh, yes," she said, with a trace of pride. "He thought himself so clever. Kept me from the outside world—but he couldn't keep the outside world from me. His precious library became my haven. The old texts, the herbals, the medical treatises. He never thought I had the mind to understand them. But I did."

She leaned in, her voice low and intimate. "I studied every word. Learned how to mimic the signs of heart failure. A little belladonna here, a tincture there. When he died, no one questioned it. Not with his 'weak heart.'"

My mouth was dry. "And Miranda?"

"Was always the end goal," she said lightly. "Once he was gone, all that lovely money would go to her. Until she turned eighteen. Then she could sign it all over to me. The will has already been written. As soon as the clock strikes midnight, she'll sign it, and then it will be delivered to our man at the bank."

She stood and paced slowly. "Once that's done, she will die."

"You're mad," I breathed.

She smiled. "No, darling. I'm Isis. The divine mother, the wife of Osiris. The one who brings life through death."

I stared at her, heart pounding. "Why are you telling me this? Aren't you afraid I'll let the world know?"

She turned toward me with a bright, terrible smile, "You won't live long enough to tell anyone."

My throat tightened.

"You will be an additional sacrifice," she said, voice now almost reverent. "A witness for the gods. The ceremony begins after midnight. As soon as Miranda signs the will, her life will end. She will be dismembered—cut into fourteen sacred pieces, just like Osiris. Her flesh sanctified. Her blood spilled in his name."

I recoiled. "You're insane."

"Perhaps," she said, unbothered. "But I will be wealthy. And free."

"You'll be hunted down," I said, forcing steel into my voice. "My husband is a chief detective inspector at Scotland

Yard. He'll see to it that justice finds you—and the rest of your cult."

Lady Fallon's expression didn't flicker. "Not me. I'll be long gone. A private plane awaits me. I'll have a new name. A new life. And a tidy sum awaiting me in an overseas account."

"You won't get your hands on it," I said. "You need more than a signature—you need access."

"Already arranged," she said coolly. "The bank officer who'll handle the transfer is a loyal member of the Osirion. As soon as Miranda is confirmed dead, the funds will be placed in my name."

"You'll never get away with this," I whispered. "You're not invincible."

Her smile deepened. "Ahh, but I am. I'm divine."

I could see it now. Truly see it. The gleam in her eyes. The unsettling calm. She didn't just believe in the cult—she believed she was its godhead.

"What will happen to me?" I asked, though I already knew.

"You will die beside her," she said gently. "Your hearts will be removed together. Your bodies broken. And then . . . the Thames will swallow you up. As if you never were."

A gong sounded in the distance.

"Ah, we're being summoned." She reached out and stroked my cheek with a touch as cold as marble. "Your time draws near, little dove. But don't worry. It won't hurt. I'll make sure of that."

And with that, she turned and glided from the room, the door slamming shut behind her with a finality that echoed in my bones.

I was alone again. Bound. Powerless.

But I was *not* finished.

Not yet.

CHAPTER 21

THE CULT OF OSIRIS

*T*he minutes ticked by with a slow, excruciating drip, the cold gnawing at my limbs as I struggled against the ropes binding my wrists. But Lady Fallon's words echoed louder than any pain.

"You will die beside her."

Her calm, bone-deep certainty was more chilling than the stone chamber that held me.

But I couldn't stop thinking. I refused to do so.

Henderson. Hassan. Richard. The cult. The Osirion. Every piece of the puzzle clicked louder in my mind with every breath.

I had to know.

When the door creaked open again, Lady Fallon returned, the lantern once more in her hand. She'd added a gold robe to her ensemble. Both garments flowing behind her like ink in a river of gold. Her expression was smug now—serene in a way only the truly unhinged could be.

I sat up slowly, my wrists still bound, my tongue heavy, but my voice clear.

"Did you kill them?" I asked.

Her brows lifted with feigned innocence. "Whom do you mean, darling?"

"Henderson. Hassan. Was it you?"

She gave a soft, lilting laugh and wandered closer, fingertips trailing along the wall like a lover's touch. "Not me, darling. That was Imhotep's doing. Our high priest."

A cold weight settled in my gut. "I thought Henderson was Imhotep."

Her lips curled. "No. He wanted to be. He fancied himself divinely chosen. But we found him lacking. Weak."

"What was he to the Cult of Osiris?" A question that needed an answer.

She tilted her head. "A means to an end. A scholar, yes. A loud one who craved notoriety more than truth. He arranged for your brother's lectures, you know. They provided a delightful cover for our practices. As long as the spotlight was on your brother, it could not be aimed at us. But when Henderson realized how popular they were, he wanted it all. The glory. The recognition. The legacy. And we couldn't have that. The last thing we wanted was attention."

My blood ran cold. "So that's why he baited Richard into that argument. At the museum reception."

"Precisely," she said with a frown. "He knew the director wouldn't tolerate a scandal, especially not in front of the foreign dignitaries who'd been invited. Henderson arranged for your brother to be dismissed so he could take over the lectures."

"But why did he have to die?"

Lady Fallon raised one painted brow. "Pride is a sin, Miss Worthington. And sins must be punished. He paid for his ambition with his life."

Her voice turned languid. "Imhotep himself saw to that."

My throat tightened. "And Hassan?"

She rolled her eyes in a gesture of theatrical exasperation. "Hassan was . . . unreliable. He could be bought and sold with a few shillings. Bribes, threats, bargains—he lacked faith. We could not afford a disciple who wasn't true to the cause."

"So, Imhotep killed him too?"

"But of course," she said as though it were obvious. "Imhotep had to cleanse the path before the resurrection. Purity of purpose is everything." She glanced around the space. "My, it's rather dark in here. Would you like some light?"

"Please."

"I can at least grant you that small wish." Suiting action to words, she used the lantern flame to light a sconce on the wall. It wasn't much. But it was better than the unrelenting darkness.

I stared at her, heart hammering. "Who is Imhotep?" Might as well ask since she was in a sharing mood.

She smiled again. Slower this time. As though savoring the moment. "In his *worldly* form, you mean."

"Yes."

She stepped closer, crouching down until we were eye to eye. Her breath was warm, scented with myrrh. "You'll find out soon enough."

My skin prickled. Every cell in my body screamed to run, to fight, to do something. But my limbs were still sluggish with whatever drug she'd used on me, and the ropes burned where I pulled too hard.

She touched my cheek with a mockery of tenderness. "He's very eager to see you, you know. You're to play an important role in Osiris's rebirth."

"I won't cooperate," I spat.

"Oh, darling," she whispered, rising to her feet. "You already are."

The door closed behind her with a soft click.

I was alone once more, with nothing but the knowledge that Henderson had been used and discarded, Hassan silenced, and Miranda—dear, terrified Miranda—was next.

Unless someone stopped them.

Unless I stopped them.

I twisted my wrists, ignoring the pain.

I had to get free.

Before Imhotep came for me.

My limbs were beginning to thaw. Not from warmth—there was none of that in this tomb-like room—but from something else. My faculties, sluggish as they were, were stirring back to life. The fog in my brain was lifting bit by bit, and with it came the return of sharp pain—my wrists bound too tightly, my body trembling with the aftershock of whatever foul mixture they had poured into my blood.

I drew in a shaky breath and looked around, trying not to move too quickly. The dim glow from the wall sconce Lady Fallon had lit barely illuminated the space. But it was enough to reveal something that sent a prickle of recognition through me.

This was the room I had hidden in when I first crept into the temple. The one filled with strange artifacts—knives, jars, ropes, incense burners, ritual instruments I couldn't begin to name. The very room where I had stumbled upon the truth and nearly been caught.

Now I was back.

And unless I did something quickly, I would not be leaving again.

With great effort, I swung my legs over the side of the high ceremonial bed. My feet hit the ground awkwardly, and my knees buckled. The room spun around me. The drug was not through with me yet. But I would not allow it to vanquish me. Too much was at stake. Gritting my teeth, I forced myself upright.

Once I got my bearings, I scanned the room for anything I could use to free myself.

A table in the center gleamed faintly. I half-stumbled, half-crawled to it, careful not to make a sound. My fingers brushed against something small and cold.

A blade. By God.

Crude but sharp. Likely ceremonial. Just what I needed.

I dropped to my knees, curling the rope upward. Sliding the blade awkwardly between the strands, I sawed back and forth. My fingers were still numb, my grip clumsy, but I kept going. I had no choice.

My wrists were raw and bleeding by the time the last strand gave way and snapped. The ropes fell to the floor.

I sucked in a breath of relief—too soon.

Footsteps.

Voices.

The door.

I climbed awkwardly onto the bed, tucking the blade behind my back. I willed my breathing to slow, my muscles to slacken. It took every ounce of control I had.

Three men entered.

Their voices were low, clipped.

"Still out."

"She'll need another dose of the elixir."

"No point. Look at her—she's not even twitching. She's gone under."

"Fine. Let's move her."

Rough hands grabbed my shoulders and feet. I fought the instinct to recoil, to strike, to scream. I tightened my fingers around the blade, even as it dug painfully into my skin. It was a risk I had to take.

They dropped me onto something hard and narrow—a litter. I stifled a sob as the blade cut into me. My head lolled to the side as they lifted it, carrying me out into the corridor beyond. I cracked my eyes open a fraction, careful to keep them glassy and unfocused.

A third man walked ahead, holding a torch.

The flame flickered off the stone walls, throwing grotesque shadows across the path. The men said nothing more. They walked with practiced purpose, as if this ceremony had been rehearsed dozens of times. Perhaps it had.

The air grew colder.

I felt it first as a prickling on my skin, then a chill that seeped deep into my bones. We had entered a larger space— vast and echoing. The scent of incense filled my nostrils: frankincense, myrrh, and something metallic beneath it all— blood, perhaps. The hairs on my arms rose.

We were in the sanctuary.

The chamber where the ceremony would take place.

New voices echoed around me—dozens, maybe more. Murmuring, chanting in low, rhythmic pulses. My skin crawled.

A fourth voice rose above the others.

"Welcome, disciples. The hour of Osiris's ascension is nearly upon us."

A hush fell.

Then I was dropped—unceremoniously—onto a flat stone slab. The cold surface bit into my back, knocking the breath from my lungs. The blade did its work again, but I was impervious to the pain.

I dared a sliver of vision.

And saw him.

Imhotep.

He stood above me in full regalia: a long black robe stitched with gold symbols, his arms bare and painted with ancient markings. A golden mask concealed his face, stylized into a serene and terrible expression—the god of the dead and rebirth. The god who demanded sacrifice.

He leaned closer, and I caught the scent of his skin through the incense.

It was subtle. Familiar.

Sandalwood, and a trace of old, dusty leather. Something I had once smelled.

Recognition struck like a slap.

I knew who he was.

Imhotep was no chosen divine. He was a man. A man I had seen before, admired for his intellect, whose presence had once seemed merely fascinating. One who'd played us all for fools.

I would unmask him.

I just needed to survive long enough to do it.

CHAPTER 22

BLOOD AND REVELATION

"*H*ello, Professor Larchmont," I said softly, my voice rasping from disuse, the chill of the stone altar biting into my back.

He gazed at me, mask glinting in the torchlight, and for a heartbeat, I saw his eyes behind it—glassy, too bright, and disturbingly calm.

"Ah," he murmured, "the maiden awakens."

"I am no maiden," I said with as much disdain as I could muster. "As you very well know."

A soft chuckle escaped him, more hollow than amused. "No matter. You are not the *one*."

His head turned slightly to the right where, I knew, Miranda waited—bound and trembling, draped in white.

"Miranda is," he said reverently. "Pure, untouched. She will make a fine *Vessel*."

We were far enough from the disciples now—those robed figures seated in rows of stools, their hands lifted in dark prayer, their chants growing louder by the moment. No one could hear our conversation over the rhythmic rise of voices, over the stifling incense smoke. But I knew. Knew it in my bones.

He meant to kill me.

He was playing with me—taunting me—as much as a cat toys with a mouse before the kill.

I flexed my fingers against the small ceremonial blade behind my back. It dug into my skin. A cruel comfort. A promise.

Could I do it?

I had defended myself before. I had fought back. But never with a blade. Never with the full, clear intent to kill.

But this was different.

Miranda's life—never mind my own—depended on it.

The chanting rose in tempo, in fervor, echoing against the high vaulted ceilings of the temple. It sounded like madness or worse. Encouragement.

From the corner of my eye, I caught movement—dozens of cloaked figures seated in ordered rows, as if they were parishioners in a church. But this was not a holy place.

It was a shrine to death.

A desecrated cathedral where they expected Osiris to be reborn, and innocence would be shattered.

"Why are you doing this?" I asked, stalling for time, voice steady despite the tremor in my chest.

Larchmont—Imhotep—turned to me fully now. His gold mask catching firelight. "Osiris must return."

"Why?" I pressed.

His hands lifted as if in benediction. "Because we have lost our way. War, disease, poverty, corruption . . . The world is crumbling. But Osiris—he is balance, resurrection, order. He will bring prosperity to the land."

"By killing an innocent girl?" I snapped.

He exhaled softly, almost a sigh. "A sacrifice is needed. To awaken the divine. To restore what has been lost."

He stepped closer. "I'm sorry you awakened," he added. "I never intended for you to suffer. But alas, the time is here."

He lifted a blade.

Long. Curved. Ritualistic.

But before it descended—before he could end me—I slid off the altar and drove my own blade into his side with everything I had.

The chanting faltered. Some cried out. Others rose in confusion.

His eyes rolled back, and he crumpled, the golden mask clattering to the ground beside him with a hollow, final sound.

Then chaos.

Whistles shrieked like banshees, and from the back of the temple came the unmistakable thunder of boots on stone. Police officers burst into the nave—helmets gleaming, pistols drawn, shouting orders.

Screams erupted from the disciples.

I could barely move. My legs buckled beneath me, the strength I'd gathered slipping away like water through a sieve.

I caught sight of Miranda, still bound. And—Lady Fallon.

She was there, screeching like a fury, her once-careful mask of elegance torn asunder by madness.

"She must die!" she screamed, lunging for Miranda with a blade in her hand. "The *Vessel* must bleed! She must die for Osiris! For me!"

The police were too far away to reach her in time.

But I was not.

I staggered forward, grabbed the nearest object—an ornate chalice from the altar, heavy, golden—and swung.

The blow struck Lady Fallon square on the temple.

She crumpled like a marionette with its strings cut.

I fell to my knees beside her, the chalice slipping from my hand, my vision tunneling into nothing but haze and smoke and the sounds of voices I could no longer follow.

Then, a pair of arms caught me—strong arms that I knew as well as my own heartbeat.

"Catherine," Robert breathed, his face pale, his eyes wide with terror. "My love."

I tried to speak. I wanted to tell him it was all right now. That Miranda was safe. That I'd stopped Imhotep. That Lady Fallon was no goddess, only a woman consumed by greed and delusion.

But the words never came.

My knees gave out fully and my head slumped against Robert's shoulder. I heard Miranda sobbing in the background, the wail of sirens in the distance. The dull thud of boots, the cries of those arrested, the metallic rasp of cuffs.

And then I sensed only darkness.

As I slipped into unconsciousness, one last thought passed through my mind—ridiculous, absurd, and thoroughly my own.

How very embarrassing of me.

CHAPTER 23

ALL'S WELL THAT ENDS WELL

With the investigation behind us, our family and dearest friends had gathered once more at Worthington House. This time not in worry or dread, but in celebration. The supper had been warm and abundant, rich with laughter and the unspoken relief that we were all, remarkably, still whole. Afterward, we drifted into the drawing room, drawn by the golden promise of firelight and the irresistible scent of toffee pudding.

There was a stillness in the air, soft and rare. Not silence, but something deeper—like the house itself had exhaled. A quiet murmur of contentment that threaded through the room.

And me—standing there with Robert's hand wrapped around mine, his thumb brushing slow circles against my skin. His presence beside me felt not only reassuring but anchoring. My heart, for the first time in what felt like ages, felt light. Unburdened. I hadn't realized until now just how much I had carried—fear, responsibility, the unrelenting urgency to fix what had gone wrong. And now, it was as though I could finally breathe.

If such a thing as a perfect evening existed, surely this was it. Not because it was extraordinary, but because it was ordinary in all the most beautiful ways: safe, warm, and filled with the people I loved.

Richard was free. Henderson's and Hassan's murderer had been apprehended. Yes, he'd lived. I was glad for I hadn't wished his death on my conscience. When interrogated by Scotland Yard, he'd admitted the attack on his person had been a ruse performed solely for Julian's benefit, whom he'd been expecting. Found guilty of the gruesome murders he'd committed, he would soon meet justice at the end of a rope.

Isis—what she called herself as she was being carted off to jail—had been temporarily committed to an asylum. Whether she would legally be determined insane remained to be seen.

Greyson and Fadil Amin had claimed they had no idea a murder would be committed that night. But the evidence found at Greyson's home and Amin's shop said otherwise. They'd both been fully aware of what the ceremony would entail. At the very least, they would spend the rest of their lives locked up behind bars.

As for the other members of the cult, the Crown Prosecution Service was still weighing charges against them. Most had attended thinking it was a lark. My guess was they would never see justice in a court of law. The court of public opinion was another thing entirely. Some had been so shamed, they'd decided to take an extended holiday somewhere very far away.

The mystery of how Henderson's remains were smuggled into the British Museum wasn't a mystery at all. His own keys had been used. Robert and I should have realized it. We didn't agonize over this lapse in judgment. Rather, we'd chalked it off to a lesson learned.

Miranda had miraculously recovered from her ordeal with barely any damage, either physical or emotional. Having been granted full control of her fortune, she'd rehired the companion her mother had dismissed. Turned out Miranda had been incredibly fond of her. Now that she was free to do as she wished, she'd decided to travel through the continent with the companion by her side, as well as an elite unit of private protection officers. Needless to say, Egypt was *not* a planned stop on their itinerary.

And as for Julian, a highly appreciative Richard had written letters of recommendation to the sponsor of his last archaeological endeavor as well as the director of the dig. Just this week, we'd heard from our dear friend. He'd been taken on as a junior member of Richard's former team. As was to be expected, he was thrilled beyond words.

The press, predictably, had sensationalized every detail— it was, after all, a scandalous story. But the frenzy would fade, as it always did, the moment a new sensation claimed their attention.

I took the newspaper accounts in stride. Not the first time I'd made the news. The notoriety brought even more business to the Ladies of Distinction Detective Agency. So much so, Emma and I were once more searching for a new lady detective. After her splendid work in the investigation, we'd promoted Mellie to Assistant Lady Detective, a position she treasured. Given our growing staff, we needed larger quarters. So, we'd signed a lease on a new address. A stunning four-story Georgian terrace building located on Essex Street, close to the Underground. Situated as it was, near the Middle Temple barristers, we were sure to encounter wigs and gowns on our future morning walks.

As for my family, a glowing Margaret sat near the hearth,

content in the knowledge that baby Thomas was in the Worthington nursery being watched over by Nanny Maude. Sebastian was at her side, proud and watchful, as though he'd personally invented fatherhood. My parents beamed at them both, though I caught Mother eyeing Richard now and then with a mother's fretful fondness, as if afraid that if she blinked, he might disappear again. She tried to apologize to me for the words she'd employed after Richard had been arrested. Embracing her, I'd brushed them aside assuring her no harm had been done.

"I must say," Father declared, holding up his glass, "I never expected to toast the return of my youngest son from the clutches of the Crown Prosecution Office, but here we are."

Richard raised his own. "To the truth. And to a sister who refused to stop digging."

I blushed and waved him off, though Robert gave my hand an affectionate squeeze. His look told me he was proud, which, frankly, meant the world to me.

In a corner sofa, Marlowe and Emma were locked in a heated debate over the last bite of toffee pudding—as though the future of the empire hung in the balance.

"It's mine," Emma said, her fork poised like a weapon.

"You didn't even want dessert," Marlowe countered, leaning in far too closely. "And now you want the very best part? Scandalous."

Emma didn't move away. Instead, she tilted her head, eyes dancing. "I always want the best part, milord. I simply wait until the very end to take it."

Marlowe's lips curled into a slow, wicked smile. "Then by all means," he said, lowering his voice, "take it. But be warned —I don't give up sweet things so easily."

She leaned in even closer, her breath brushing his cheek. "Neither do I."

I arched a brow in Robert's direction.

He caught my look and smothered a grin. "When is their wedding?"

"Not soon enough," I replied.

Mellie and Lily swept into the room at that moment, looking like fashion plates fresh from a salon. Cheeks flushed from laughter, Lily made a beeline for Ned, who was sipping brandy near the window and pretending not to eavesdrop.

"I heard," Lily said, her eyes sparkling, "that you made quite the convincing gigolo."

Ned choked on his drink. "Who told you that?"

"Me," Mellie chimed in helpfully.

"Well, it was undercover work," he muttered, suddenly very interested in his cufflinks.

Lily leaned closer, playful and wicked. "Will you escort me somewhere as one? Somewhere scandalous. Dinner and dancing, perhaps. I'll wear a particularly fetching gown."

He blinked. "You want me to take you out as—?"

"A gigolo. Yes." She grinned. "I believe you owe me a scandal."

His ears went crimson, but his smile turned wicked. "I accept. But only if I get to choose the club."

"Done."

I turned to Robert with a grin. "I do believe we've started something."

He chuckled, pulling me closer. "We're a bad influence." He didn't appear the least bit penitent.

Across the room, Richard was holding court now, his glass raised again as he answered yet another question about what came next. "I've been offered a summer lectureship at Oxford," he said, almost shyly. "It's informal at the moment— just a series of talks—but they're hinting at something more permanent come autumn. Apparently, my experience has become . . . invaluable."

"After all that business at the British Museum," Emma said, "you're practically famous."

"They expect my lectures to be well-attended," Richard admitted with an amused smile. "Though I expect most will attend to see if I'm arrested mid-sentence."

"If you are," Father said, "do let us know in advance. We'll sell tickets."

That earned a fresh round of laughter, just as our butler entered with a silver tray and a telegram.

"For Lady Melissande."

"Thank you, Carlton." A frowning Mellie took the envelope, her fingers hesitating a moment before tearing it open. Her eyes scanned the page once, then twice. Her lips parted, then pressed into a thin line.

"Well?" I asked, curiosity piqued.

She handed it to me.

As I read the telegram, my mouth dropped open. "That's it? After disappearing, all we get from Hollingsworth is *In Madeira. Am well?*"

"I'm going to wring his neck when I see him again," Mellie muttered.

There was a beat of stunned silence. And then—laughter. Loud and genuine and unstoppable. Even Mother had to dab her eyes.

"He's alive," Robert said gently. "And he reached out. That's more than we had yesterday."

"True," Mellie sighed. "But I still might wring his neck."

The room began to settle again, people pairing off, conversations ebbing and flowing like music. Robert drew me aside toward the window, where the moon was rising above the garden in soft, silvery light.

"It's over," I whispered. "At least this part of it."

He turned me to face him, brushing a stray curl from my

cheek. "For now. Until the next mystery knocks on our door."

"Or breaks it down."

His smile warmed me to my toes. "Whatever comes, Catherine, I have no doubt we'll face it together."

And as the warmth of family laughter surrounded us and the moon watched from above, I felt—for the first time in weeks—that we were precisely where we were meant to be.

Together.

Alive.

And ready for whatever adventure came next.

DID you enjoy **Murder at the British Museum?** Read on to discover Kitty Worthington's next adventure.

A Murder on London Bridge

TWO TIMELINES. **One murder. A mystery that burns through the ages.**

London. 1925. Now settled into their married lives, **Kitty**

Worthington and her husband, Robert Crawford Sinclair, are thrilled to host their first formal dinner. Among their guests is an antiquities dealer who hints at a groundbreaking discovery, a document so important it's bound to ruin lives. Days later, the dealer is bludgeoned to death on London Bridge.

Plunged into a mystery of historical proportions, Kitty embarks on a quest for the truth. Her search uncovers a cryptic manuscript hinting at a shadowy Stuart-era society. As the stakes rise, an ancient historian warns Kitty that digging too deep can be deadly. Undeterred, she presses on, only to be struck down as well.

1666. Kitty awakens to find herself in the court of **King Charles II**, serving as a lady-in-waiting to the Queen Consort Catherine of Braganza. Even as she navigates courtly intrigue and a growing danger to the queen's life, London erupts in flames. Trapped in the past with the Great Fire blazing around her, will Kitty find her way back, or is she doomed to perish in history's ashes?

A Murder on London Bridge, Book 13 in The Kitty Worthington Mysteries, is another captivating historical cozy mystery from the pen of *USA Today* Bestselling Author Magda Alexander. This gripping dual-timeline mystery will transport you through danger, intrigue, and the flames of history—one twist at a time.

CURIOUS ABOUT LORD Hollingsworth's whereabouts? I certainly was. After much arm twisting, metaphorically speaking, of course, he finally told me what he's been up to.

. . .

AFTER A DEVASTATING INJURY ends his career at sea, Lord Hollingsworth retreats to Madeira, burdened by loss and doubt. There, he meets Isabel Montrose--a spirited widow with her own scars--and an unexpected bond begins to heal them both. But when a violent storm strikes, Hollingsworth must face the ultimate test: will he surrender to the past, or reclaim the life--and love--he thought forever lost?

You can download **Hollingsworth's Lost Horizon**, by clicking the link below:

https://dl.bookfunnel.com/c2hvccpsxk

CAST OF CHARACTERS

Kitty Worthington - Our sleuth

The Crawford Sinclair Family

Robert Crawford Sinclair - Kitty's husband, a Scotland Yard Detective Chief Inspector. Recently inherited the Lord Rutledge marquessate title

The Crawford Sinclair Household

Mister Black - the Crawford Sinclair Butler
Hudson - Robert's valet
Grace Flanagan- Kitty's Lady's Maid

The Worthington Family

Mildred Worthington - Kitty's mother
Edward Worthington - Kitty's father
Ned Worthington - Kitty's oldest brother, engaged to Lily Dalrymple

Richard Worthington - Kitty's next oldest brother, formerly in Egypt now in London

The Worthington Household

Carlton - the family butler
Neville - the family chauffeur and Betsy's fiancé
Sir Winston - Family's beloved basset hound

The Ladies of Distinction Detective Agency

Lady Emma Carlyle - Kitty's friend and partner in the Ladies of Distinction Detective Agency, engaged to Lord Marlowe

Lady Aurelia Holmes - Assistant lady detective

Betsy Robson - Receptionist and assistant bookkeeper at the Ladies of Distinction Detective Agency, formerly Kitty's personal maid, engaged to Neville, the Worthington family chauffeur

Owen Clapham - Former Scotland Yard detective inspector, aids with investigations

The Wynchcombe Family and Household

His Grace the Duke of Wynchcombe, Sebastian Dalrymple - married to Margaret, Kitty's sister

Her Grace the Duchess of Wynchcombe, Margaret Dalrymple - Kitty's older sister, now married to the Duke of Wynchcombe

Lady Lily Dalrymple - Sebastian's sister, engaged to Ned, Kitty's brother, currently living with the Worthington family

Other Notable Characters

Lord Hollingsworth - A Marquis, Explorer, and Adventurer, and Robert Crawford Sinclair's best mate, Lady Melissande's brother

Lady Melissande ("Mellie") - Lord Hollingsworth's sister, currently living with the Worthington family, newest Assistant Lady Detective trainee

Lord Marlowe - An Earl - Engaged to Lady Emma

Julian Banks – A recent Oxford graduate

Lady Hutton - a client of the Ladies of Distinction Detective Agency

Lady Miranda - Lady Hutton's daughter

Doctor Martin Henderson - Curator of Egyptian Antiquities at the British Museum

Mister Branson - Assistant to Richard Worthington

Professor Larchmont - Egyptian Scholar

ISBN-13: (EBook) 978-1-943321-37-7

ISBN-13: (Print) 978-1-943321-47-6

Hearts Afire Publishing

First Edition: April 2025